LOVER'S KNOT

KAREN CHANCE

Spoiler warning: This novella is part of the Dorina Basarab series of books. It is set after the first three novels in the series, *Midnight's Daughter*, *Death's Mistress*, and *Fury's Kiss*, and contains spoilers for those books.

CHAPTER ONE

1457, Mircea
The rooftops of Venice, Italy

Something hit the side of a building and exploded, sending dagger-like pieces of brick flying outwards. One cut Mircea's cheek, even in the split second it took for him to race by at vampire speed. He bit back a curse and then wondered why he bothered. Blood was a siren's song to his ears, and likely louder still to his pursuers.

But he and his companion were already covered in it.

A stray beam of moonlight lit the tumbled blond hair and ivory features of the vampire Mircea was now less supporting than outright carrying. It also highlighted the fear in his eyes, because Jerome could sense their pursuers, too. And the fact that they were closing in.

"Leave me," he whispered, barely a sigh on the wind. But right on cue, two more shadows altered course, converging on their position from several streets over. Or several canals, which were the only thing that had saved them so far. Walking on water was a skill set reserved for the undamned part of humanity, of which neither they nor their pursuers could number themselves any longer.

But it wasn't going to be enough.

Mircea could see it in the slow but steady gain the leaders were making. Could taste it in the difference in the age and quality of the blood flowing through their veins, and that trickling down his own face. Could feel it every time one of those strange energy bolts they were throwing exploded against a building or hissed through the water in a canal. Only a superior knowledge of the city had kept him alive this long.

Alive, he thought derisively, a bitter gorge rising in his throat even as he leaped from the side of a canal. He hadn't been alive for years now, as evidenced by the fact that, instead of taking a bath in the dirty water, his foot hit the bottom of a passing barge, using it as a springboard to the side of a building on the opposite shore. But he wasn't ready to go into the great unknown that followed death just yet, either, although that was starting to look like an inevitability.

At least, it was if he stayed on the ground.

"Hold on," he told Jerome, and jumped for the roof.

There was a brief, very un-vampire-like scramble for purchase on crumbling brick, before his foot finally caught a piece of masonry that didn't disintegrate under his heel. His free hand grabbed a gutter, his other foot found the top of a window, and there. Suddenly, they were tearing across the rain-slick rooftops of Venice, terracotta sliding under Mircea's feet as he fought for balance and speed.

And he wasn't the only one. The vampires were right behind them, dark, barely visible silhouettes against the star-strewn sky that were rapidly getting bigger. Because the ruse hadn't worked.

"Leave me!" Jerome said again, grabbing the front of Mircea's shirt.

"Be silent," Mircea hissed, wishing passionately for a sword. But swords and armor were from his old life, and wouldn't help him now. Not when all the rules had changed, and everything he'd ever been taught about life upended.

Well, almost everything.

"What are you doing?" Jerome whispered as Mircea grabbed the heavy coin purse off his companion's belt. And bounded to a house across a narrow alley. And scrambled over the pitch of the roof to stare down at the brilliantly lit square below, which was flooded with revelers now that the earlier squalls had dissipated.

5

"Mircea..."

"Buying time," Mircea said, and threw a glittering arc into the teeming crowd.

A moment later, he and Jerome landed in the middle of the yelling, scuffling, gold-maddened throng, along with a dozen shadows he could barely see, but not because of anything they were doing.

But because the square was dazzling.

The quiet, moon-drenched canals had suddenly been replaced by a dizzying kaleidoscope of senses. Light streamed across Mircea's vision from torches and windows and lanterns and candles. Sound hit his ears like battlefield bombardment, full of shouts and squeals, calls and curses. Scuffling feet and flying elbows were everywhere, along with gleaming dark eyes behind leering masks, and glittering jeweled necks, and reaching dirty hands, and incense and mildew and bad breath and alcohol. Even for a human, it would have been stunning; for someone with a vampire's abilities, it was like being hit with a fist, disorienting as all hell.

Mircea badly needed a moment.

But he didn't have one, because that was the point: to lead his pursuers somewhere where their elevated senses would actually work against them. So he pushed forward, onto a side street, while hunching over and throwing his cape across Jerome. And hoping that nobody had gotten a good look at him.

But they'd certainly gotten a good smell.

Smell *this*, Mircea thought, as a hand like a vise grabbed his arm, and he grabbed minds in houses all along the narrow street. Shutters slammed open, people appeared on balconies, and a rain of trash started pelting down all around them. Old fish heads, rotting vegetables, and the contents of a day's worth of chamber pots filled the skies and splattered the already rain-slick streets, sending beautifully dressed revelers slipping and sliding and screaming invective. And Mircea tearing away from his pursuer in the chaos.

If they didn't want us dead before, they do now, Jerome sent him mentally, as another vampire lunged for them. Only to be hit by a fetid stream from above that soaked his clothes and sent his feet flying out from under him.

But he was the only one. The others were briefly held up by the crowd's churning outrage, but they were still coming. His trick had bought seconds only, and Mircea couldn't pull a stunt like that again. As it was, controlling that many minds at once had his vision pulsing in and out and his heart pounding as it hadn't in a decade.

What a time to feel human again, he thought grimly, and darted down another street, this one filled with fishermen.

They were coming in from a long day on the boats and cutting an odorous swath through the glittering throng. Mircea dove through a cloud reeking of their trade, overlaid with stale sweat, cheap wine, and rotting teeth. And then into another composed of frying oil and *frittelle* from a peddler's cart, pungent with vanilla and orange. And finally into a perfume explosion around a crowd of yellow-garbed girls, in the particular hue that Venice reserved for its whores.

One of them stuck a flower behind his ear when he paused to stare around. "*Bona fortuna*," she laughed, and kissed him.

The low-cut top of her dress showed off a chest as flat as a boy's, belying the promise of carmine lips and kohl-rimmed eyes.

She looked all of about twelve.

She wasn't.

The dark-haired beauty had been plying her trade since Romulus was suckling on a hairy teat, as evidenced by the strength of the slender hand that gripped his arm. And by the mental command that he couldn't hear, because he wasn't a master, and it wasn't directed at him. But which caused a cascade of silks to flutter into the street behind them.

"Marsilia," Mircea gasped, in considerable relief.

"My girls can't hold them for long," she told him quickly. "Get to the square; I'll send help to you there."

He nodded and pulled Jerome forward while a commotion

started up behind them. It wasn't a fight, just a line of laughing girls playing one of the pranks carnival was famous for, and blocking the path. Of course, the crowd was doing the same thing to him, battering him on all sides, and pushing him and Jerome toward the edge of a canal. Where a smear of golden fire from a string of bobbing lanterns illuminated a floating, flower-festooned parade.

Venice's high society was packed into boats along with their trains of hangers-on, sycophants, and bodyguards, none of whom reacted to having two panicked vampires plow through their midst. Because Mircea made sure that they were gone before their presence even registered, leaping from boat to boat to boat, working their way around the blockage. And then running down a narrow alley, before spilling out into the great square beside St. Mark's.

Mircea paused, both because Jerome had just become a complete dead weight, falling into a healing trance in a last-ditch effort to save himself. And because, ahead of them, was a working sea of people: thousands, maybe tens of thousands, filling the huge square to the brim and running over. And packed so tightly, Mircea doubted he could have gotten a piece of paper in between them.

It would have been perfect—if he and Jerome had been on the other side. As it was, there was no chance of battling their way through before their pursuers caught up. No chance at all.

His head tilted back.

Well, except for maybe one.

And then a leering jester jumped at him out of the crowd, right in his face. Mircea flinched back before the exaggerated mask was pushed up, leaving him looking at the broad, familiar features of Nicolò, Marsilia's right-hand man. The dimpled face under the mop of curly dark hair was usually grinning, to the point that people forgot how truly vicious he could be.

He wasn't grinning now.

"How many?" Mircea yelled, the roar of the crowd making discretion impossible, and probably unnecessary.

"Fifteen."

"Fifteen?"

"That we've counted so far—"

"And your men can't take that many," Mircea finished for him, because it wasn't even a question.

Nicolò shook his head. "Not with a master among them, second level at a guess."

Mircea swallowed. A second-level master was basically an army all on his own. But at least it explained how Jerome had ended up gutted. He was a master himself, as far above Mircea's limited abilities as Mircea was to a human. Strong enough that he hadn't bothered with bodyguards.

Might want to rethink that decision, Mircea thought, and pushed him at Nicolò.

"And what do I do with this?" the larger vamp demanded.

"Take him to my house! I'll meet you there."

The curly head shook again. "I told you, we'll never make it —"

"I'll provide a distraction!"

"Better be a hell of a distraction," Nicolò muttered and grabbed a barrel off a passing cart. He cracked it open like an egg, drenching both himself and Jerome in the process, and covering the scent of blood with the acrid tang of cheap wine. "Now we smell like everyone else," Nicolò yelled.

And abruptly jerked his head around.

Mircea followed his gaze to see Jerome's pursuers running full tilt down the alley. But not because the crowd had suddenly thinned, but because they had gotten on top of the problem—literally. They were sprinting above the multitude, on shoulders, backs, and even heads, using the densely packed revelers like rocks in a stream, and as a shortcut to the square.

"Whatever you're going to do, now would be good," Nicolò said—from behind him. Because Mircea had already taken off, ripping the blood-soaked shirt from his back and flying it above his head. And then above the crowd, as he took a page from the vamps' book, and vaulted on top of the throng.

These people didn't seem as drunk and oblivious as those in the alley, but Mircea didn't give them time to complain. He leapt from strong back to strong back, and then from horseback to horseback, skipping down a processional line and narrowly avoiding a knight's mailed fist. He jumped to a palanquin bearing the effigy of some saint, crossed himself for the sacrilege before laughing at how stupid that was, and then laughed some more as the crowd opened up a bit and he hit solid ground again.

He sounded frankly demented, but he didn't care.

Because he could finally *move*, unfettered and unburdened, and it felt wonderful.

At least, it did until he reached the towering shadow of the campanile, the huge bell tower overlooking the square, with an army of shadows converging on him. Mircea hadn't been moving slowly before, but the wind of his passing now fluttered hair and widened eyes, causing heads to turn to try and see what was no longer there. Like that of the guard at the tower door, who blinked and missed the blur that ran past him and up the stairs.

The roar of the crowd was suddenly muffled, cut off by the heavy brick walls. Enough that Mircea could hear the almost silent footfalls behind him, could feel the subtle vibrations of their tread on the steps below. He ignored them, knowing that if he paused, even for a moment, he was lost. So he tore up the narrow, winding staircase, running full-out, while his pursuers pounded at his heels, while they grabbed at his clothes, while he slammed a foot into someone's face and heard him curse—

And then he was out the top, tearing across the checkered floor of the highest story. And to the columned opening overlooking the crowd. And the one chance he'd seen below: the thin rope used by Turkish acrobats who delighted carnival goers every year by walking up, up, up to the top of the bell tower, balance pole in hand, from a platform far out in the bay.

Mircea didn't have a pole, but he did have a blood-slick shirt. He twisted it into a chord and flung it over the heavily slanted rope, as half a dozen vampires piled up on each other at the narrow opening of the stairs. Dizzyingly far below, the crowd looked up, their attention drawn by the bell hit by one of those strange energy bolts that had been thrown at Mircea's head. It was the Malificio, the one usually rung when an execution was about to take place.

How fitting, he thought, as the snarl of vamps released, sending them stumbling onto the tiles behind him.

"*A Carnevale ogni scherzo vale**," he told them.

And jumped.

----

*"At Carnival, anything goes."

CHAPTER TWO

Present day, Dory
A floral boudoir in upstate New York

I stumbled hard and went down to one knee, before my hand grasped some expensive blue-and-white wallpaper. I stared at it blankly, while the lines of little flowers and ribbons and bows danced in front of my vision. And my brain finally got its shit together and identified them.

Of course.

Home was an old, paint-splattered, slightly dusty bedroom in a sagging matriarch of a house in Brooklyn. This place belonged to my boyfriend—if you could use that word for someone four centuries old. I knew that because I'd been here a week ago, when he unveiled the homage to the Rococo that his designer had put together for me, after steadfastly ignoring his boss's comment that my favorite color was black.

My favorite color was now blue, white, pink, and bright sunny yellow. And I apparently enjoyed it festooned with lace and feminine doodads. It was pretty damned hideous, which was why I distinctly remembered nodding and smiling and getting the heck out of dodge as quickly as possible.

Only now I was back.

For some reason.

I shook my head, trying to clear it, but it didn't help. I kept wanting to see a wintry carnival, fogged by the breath of a massive crowd, full of light, color, and noise. And stilt walkers with huge, painted heads, and people leaning out of windows to toss handfuls of sweets to too-drunk-to-catch-them revelers, and three bands trying to outdo one another and just adding to the din.

And my father, tear-assing above it all, a pack of masters at his back, laughing like a madman.

A new wave of disorientation hit me, and I decided to graduate from clutching the wall to lying face down on the carpet. I closed my eyes and breathed in the fibers of a new-smelling rug, and slowly began to feel a little better. Enough to eventually notice other smells permeating the air of my big walk-in closet.

Some of them were expected: the enthusiastically applied lemon oil on the antique furniture in the bedroom, the stuff the staff used on the sheets to make them cloud soft and smell like a summer breeze, and the sachets the maids insisted on sticking everywhere, despite my pointing out that sneaking up on bad guys was a little hard when I smelled like a lavender field.

Other smells, however, were less expected. Like a wedge of my world that had intruded into the gleaming perfection: sweaty, frightened, panicky scents that the lavender was battling, but not defeating. Because it was a constant, while the others...

Kept on coming.

I cracked open a gummy eyelid.

A bunch of terrified people were huddled in the corner of the closet, regarding me like I was the Anti-Christ.

I shut my eye again.

You know, you'd think I'd be used to this by now. Being a dhampir, the half-human, half-vampire, all-screwed-up version of humanity that I was, came with issues. Not least of which was going batshit crazy on a regular basis. That meant I had plenty of experience waking up in stranger places than a flowery boudoir, trying to handle the confusion of yet another foray into the weirdness that was my life. Sometimes, I really thought—

Somebody gave a little scream.

I sighed and opened my eyes again.

And saw a woman—the one who'd screamed at a guess—

trying to forge a path through the crowd to the back, only to discover that no one would let her in. That seemed to up the ante on the whole terror thing, leaving her plastered to the wall of people now all trying to hide behind each other. While yelling.

I blinked at them, and then at my reflection in a nearby, floor-length mirror. Yes, dhampirs are the bogeymen—and women—of the vampire world, but right now, I wasn't doing much to uphold standards. The cap of short, dark hair was the same, as were the black eyes looking in confusion out of a face that should have been pleasingly olive, but was vamp-pale thanks to the whole daddy-was-a-bloodsucking-monster thing. But they were the only similarities.

Because my butt was in the air, my cheek was on the floor, and I was lacking my usual well-oiled accessories.

All of them.

My jeans, leather jacket, and butt-kicking boots had been replaced by a frilly scrap of silk pretending to be a nightgown. It matched the thong wedged up the aforementioned butt and was courtesy of the aforementioned boyfriend. Who had been born when men wore silks and laces, but who'd realized at some point that these things weren't considered manly in the 21st century.

So he'd started dumping them on me.

I would have had more to say about that, but the bastard could be persuasive. Like proffering the ridiculous nightwear on one finger, while prowling toward me with exactly nothing at all covering those hard muscles and sleek lines. And while those aristocratic features took on the half-heated, half-amused look he got when he was about to—

But that wasn't the point here.

The point was the group of terrified people crowding my closet.

I sat up.

"Ahhh! Ahhh!"

"Help us, oh Jesus!"

"Let me through, let me through!"

"I was here first!"

I grabbed my head because it hurt. A lot. And the screaming wasn't helping.

"Shut up!" I finally yelled.

There was sudden, blissful silence.

And then somebody made a break for the door.

And despite some middle-aged pudge and a pair of sagging, sans-a-belt slacks, it was a fast break, because he was a vamp. At least, I was pretty sure. I caught him by the leg and jerked him down.

Little fangs, bared in what looked like terror. A pulse beating frantically in his too pale neck, because he hadn't learned that he didn't need it yet. Wildly fluctuating power surges, if you could dignify the amount of energy he was giving off by that name. Skin far too cold, because he hadn't eaten recently, and he needed to.

Because he wasn't just a vampire.

He was a *baby*.

They all were, I realized slowly, raising my head to survey them again. What were a bunch of baby vamps doing in my closet? And, for that matter, what was I?

"Stop that," I slurred at the ravenous infant, who appeared to be trying to gnaw off my arm.

Smacking his head away, I used the pudge as leverage to get back to my feet. The babies took a collective step back, which was a good trick considering that they were already hugging the wall. I surveyed them for a second, seeing the whites around their eyes, the panicked little breaths they didn't need fluttering their clothes, and the tendency to lash out at each other like a pack of snarling dogs. I didn't know where the hell their minders were, but I couldn't very well leave them here. They might trash all this expensive frilly stuff and then that . . .

Well, that would be a shame.

I let myself dream for a moment before coming back down to earth. The designer was still around and might come up with something even worse next time. And the babies might rip each other to shreds in the process, and then I'd feel bad.

You know. Probably.

I sighed.

"All right, all of you. Out."

They got out.

"And stay together!" I yelled as they stampeded through the bedroom and out the door to the hall. "Single file, down to the kitchen. Don't make me come after you!"

I dragged the pudgy one with me, because he was easily the most far gone of the lot. Baby vamps were like baby humans; they needed to be fed on a regular basis, or bad things happened. Only these bad things hurt like a *bitch*.

I finally got all of Pudgy's pointy bits facing outward and frog-marched him downstairs to the vast, brand-new, ultra-modern kitchen that didn't go at all with the Old World atmosphere of the rest of this place. Louis-Cesare, the boyfriend in question, had his main court in France. But due to some recent political maneuvering, he'd found himself part of the North American Vampire Senate instead of the European one, so a new court had been required. Only it looked like he'd brought the other one here, stone by stone, because this place did not reflect the usual architecture of upstate New York.

Except for the kitchen.

The old stone countertops and big wooden table I'd seen on my first visit had been upgraded to the galley of the Starship Enterprise. If it was shiny, stainless steel, or high tech, the chef had it in spades. And he obviously didn't like having his pristine command center sullied by a bunch of snarling baby monsters.

"Lady Dorina! I must protest!"

"Dory," I told him, for something like the tenth time. "And where are the minders?"

I was talking about the older vamps who acted as nursemaids for the fanged tots. At least they did in most families. I hadn't been around this one long enough to find out how they dealt with their babies, or why Louis-Cesare's paternal instincts had kicked in to the tune of whatever-tuplets it is when you have a couple dozen of them.

Herd, I thought, watching the babies stagger around, and jump back from their own reflections in the shiny surfaces, because their VampVision™ didn't work properly yet. The zoom feature could send buildings, people, and fridges suddenly speeding toward them like a freight train. Or like an out-of-control dhampir, which might explain some of the screaming earlier.

"We're working on it," the harassed chef told me. Verrell was a Chef Boyardee clone with a food-appreciative gut and big dark eyes. They matched the curls escaping from under his toque, and the so-French-it-hurt little stash on his upper lip. He slammed a rolling pin down on a countertop, and a baby vamp snatched his hand back.

And started to cry.

"Mon Dieu," the chef muttered, and looked mournfully at me.

"Tell me about it," I said, while struggling with the vamp I'd decided to rename Bitey. "Or, better yet, tell Louis-Cesare. Where is he?"

"Paris."

"Paris?"

Verrell nodded in what looked like envy. "He left yesterday, in ze great hurry."

"You mean . . . Paris, France?"

Verrell blinked in confusion. "Zere is anozzer?"

Yeah, but I doubted Louis-Cesare had suddenly gotten a hankering to visit Texas. "Did he say why?"

"You 'ave to ask?" He waved a spoon around crazily. "Ze senate, zey dump all zese babies on us, wiz no warning, and wiz ze house in such a state—"

That state apparently being pristine mansion, because I'd yet to see so much as a speck of dust anywhere. I vaguely wondered what Verrell had thought of my place when he'd visited. I decided not to ask.

"The senate?" I said instead. "Then these aren't Louis-Cesare's?"

Verrell wrinkled his nose and pried a young blonde out of his truffle drawer. She had wild eyes and a jam and truffle-wreathed mouth, and Verrell regarded her with disdain. "We are not one of zose families. We 'ave ze standards."

I gave up. "When will Louis-Cesare be back?"

"If he is smart? Nevair," the chef muttered, and released the girl in order to dive after a couple of vamps who were destroying his pantry.

It wasn't unusual at that age: they needed food, their starvation-addled brains knew that much. But in their current state, they couldn't think well enough to remember that the normal stuff wouldn't help anymore. No matter how much of it they ate, I thought, watching as thousands of dollars' worth of caviar, fine oysters, and well-aged cheese went down hatches to stomachs that didn't know what to do with it anymore. The remainder splattered everywhere, causing the chef to go ballistic with the rolling pin, along with his two white-garbed helpers.

"We need to contain them somewhere!" I said, and got only crazed looks in return. Because yeah. It was like herding cats.

"Where?"

"You don't have *minders*?"

"Zey 'ave not arrived yet—"

"Then a room—a shielded one," I added, because otherwise, they'd claw through the damned plaster.

"Eet won't help," Verrell told me dolefully. "Zey are babies. Zere power ees too . . ." He waved his hands around. "Unstable, yes?"

"So?"

"So, 'ow do you set zee ward? Too low and zey walk right through eet, when zere power spikes. Too high and—zee bug zappair."

"The what?"

"Like at zee picnic, *comprenez-vous*?"

"No."

Verrell suddenly started twitching and flailing about, wildly enough that even a couple of the babies paused to stare at him. And then he stopped to do the same to me. "Zappair, zappair! Zee leetle bug, it gets too close and—" More flailing.

Light dawned. "And we don't want to zappair the babies."

Verrell's pink lips pursed.

It looked like he was thinking about it.

It didn't help that, as the minutes stretched from their last feeding, more and more of the babies were losing it. New vamps are half crazy anyway, and that's when they're well-fed. Starving ones . . .

Starving wasn't good.

Some were tearing open cabinets, stuffing their faces, and cutting their lips because they hadn't remembered to retract their fangs. Others were sitting in widening puddles of wine and melting ice cream, crying because the hunger wouldn't abate. Still others had reached the crazy stage, like Bitey, forcing me to keep hold of him while he snapped and snarled and tried to eat anyone within reach.

Like the vision in blue satin who appeared in the doorway a moment later, regarding the panting mass of hate in my arms with a slightly raised eyebrow.

"Oh, there you are, Dory. I've been looking everywhere."

"Radu, would you please—"

I tried to pass the crazed thing in my arms to Louis-Cesare's Sire, so I could help round up the others, but he wasn't having it. "My dear. He's drooling."

"I know he's drooling! He's also trying to bite my arm off!"

"He probably needs to be fed."

"I know he needs to be fed!"

"There's no reason to shout," Radu said mildly, as he swanned through the mess, wafting away snarling babies with a few motions of his well-manicured hands, in order to reach the house phone.

Why he needed it, I didn't know. With his long, shiny dark hair, satin-draped body, and languid stroll, he looked like a male supermodel freshly arrived from the seventeenth century. But behind those limpid, turquoise eyes was the mind of a second-level master vamp, meaning that he could communicate mentally with almost anyone he chose.

Except for them, I realized a moment later, when a bunch of human servants came running through the main door.

And then just as quickly turned and started out again, because 'Du had forgotten one little thing.

"No, no, no," he said crossly, as the babies stampeded by him. "Gently!"

But the babies weren't interested in gentle; the babies were interested in blood. And the fact that there was plenty to go around, and that it was being freely offered, didn't matter to creatures more or less out of their minds. Shit, I thought, and threw Bitey at them.

"Get out!" I yelled, while Bitey took out half a dozen of his friends in a crazed frenzy, sending them staggering and stumbling and sliding on the ice cream-slick floor. They went down like a bunch of bowling pins, but the rest were still coming, launching themselves with blood-crazed madness at the now petrified human servants. Who were used to donating blood, but not to being hunted by what amounted to a pack of salivating wolves.

"Go!" I repeated, with a vamp in either hand, while trying to block access to the door by wedging myself between the wall and the nearest counter. But the babies outnumbered me, and they were rapidly losing their fear to blood madness. I roared at them, an ear-shattering sound that bared my own tiny fangs, and caused a few of the still-somewhat-rational ones to rear back in alarm, only to get trampled by the crazies behind.

And then it got worse.

The tall, muscly blond whom Radu usually introduced as his bodyguard, despite the rolled eyes that produced, came through the door. But Gunther wasn't all blond good looks; he could fight, too, which is why I assumed he'd just pulled a knife. Until the knife went in his tanned forearm, and a dish towel soaked up the bright splatter it produced. And every baby's nose in the place suddenly turned up at the scent of warm, fresh, life-giving—

"Blood," Bitey growled, and tore out of my grip.

He leapt over a counter, following the blood-soaked rag, and the human waving it like a red flag in front of a whole herd of bulls. And the others followed. Including the two I had in hand, who almost towed me over the counter before I released them.

"In here!" The chef panted, jerking open a large door I hadn't noticed, because the stainless all tended to melt together. In went the rag, while Gunther ducked behind the chef's two assistants, who cut off the babies and herded them toward the door.

And then through it, before the chef slammed it shut behind them, and threw the latch.

And then looked at me and screamed, flailing his chubby hands around, because I don't think this sort of thing was on his usual agenda.

I stared back, still half-draped over the counter, but I wasn't looking at him. I was looking behind him, to where Gunther was trying to staunch the blood flowing down his arm. And seeing him again, holding the dishtowel high over his head, and running like a madman—

A cold wind swept across the kitchen, ruffling my hair and sending goosebumps sliding up my arms. My eyes crossed as they tried to take in two different places at once. And two different times.

"Well, shit," I said thickly, and fell over.

CHAPTER THREE

1457, Mircea
A tiny wart of a house in Venice, Italy

R ain lashed the little structure, sending it shuddering as if in pain with every gust. Mircea ignored it, concentrating on Jerome, who was never going to heal if he kept bleeding like a stuck pig. But it was hard to avoid that when half your guts were on the floor, like bloody worms scrawling over the stained wood. And Mircea couldn't put them back where they belonged, because Jerome had come out of his trance and was fighting him—

And he was fighting hard.

A delirious master vampire is one of the deadliest creatures on Earth. As demonstrated when Mircea was thrown across the room, hitting the wall and then landing in a sprawl of paint and canvas. So much for his latest artistic effort, he thought, and flung it at Jerome. Not because it would help, but because he didn't have anything else.

But the distraction was seized by Nicolò, who slammed a meaty fist into the side of Jerome's blond head a second later, only to go sailing himself. Through the side of the house, and into the wildly frothing waters of the sea outside, making a new entrance in the process. Several of the other vamps just stood there, staring after him, while another ran wildly for the front door.

Mircea couldn't really blame him.

He swallowed, staring at Jerome's bloody face, at glowing copper eyes and long, bared fangs, and wondered if this had been the best idea. Even Marsilia, who had shown up a couple of minutes before, was now plastered against the wall, waiting for him to do something. Because age doesn't always equal power, and even after all these years, she was barely a master. While Jerome... well, Mircea wasn't sure what his level was, but it was safe to say it was higher than theirs.

And then he lunged.

Several vamps dove out of the way, Mircea threw out a hand, trying vainly to get into Jerome's deranged brain, and Marsilia screamed.

And then, suddenly, everything stopped.

For a second, all Mircea saw was a tableaux worthy of artists who commanded much higher fees than he: vamps hugging the walls or desperately trying to fit through the door; a dripping Nicolò, pausing half in, half out of the wall, his face furious; Marsilia, her ruby lips parted in shock; Horatiu, Mircea's old manservant, silhouetted in the door to the kitchen, his gnarled hand clutching a frying pan.

And a tiny, barefoot child in a white chemise, one still too long for her because Mircea had gotten it from a second-hand stall, standing on the stairs.

Jerome paused, bloody mouth agape, and stared at the girl. She looked like a tiny angel, her long dark hair a sleep-rumpled mass tumbling to her waist, her dark eyes large and watchful, her cheeks pale but her lips pink. Mircea's heart leaped to his throat because of all his nightmares, this was the worst. He tensed, ready to throw himself at his friend, ready to kill or die, ready to do anything to save her—

"Stop it," she told Jerome, frowning.

And Jerome stopped. All of a sudden, the fight seemed to flood out of him, like the blood that stained the floor where he collapsed. For a second, the whole room just stared.

And then everything snapped back into full color and speed.

Mircea grabbed his daughter, hugging her to him, while every other vampire in the place gazed at them in shock, the spine-tingling *run-run-run* feeling of their only natural predator screaming in the air around them. Mircea swallowed again, but looked back defiantly. And wondered what happened now.

❖ ❖ ❖

"Dhampir." Nicolò said nothing else, but he didn't need to. It was all in his eyes, the same mix of emotion that Mircea had encountered every time he'd heard that word. It had been hard to accept that the daughter he cherished was considered a monster by the people of his new world, and viewed the same way that humans viewed them: with anger, loathing, hatred.

And fear.

Mircea was trying to sew up a newly meek Jerome, but it was slow going, with Nicolò hulking over them and staring at Dorina. She was by the kitchen wall now, dabbing on a piece of paper with some charcoal, seemingly unconcerned by the bevy of fanged creatures around her. The other vampires were on the other side of the room, supposedly spreading a sheet over the unexpected doorway, but in reality getting as far from the child as possible.

Except for Nicolò.

Mircea's hand was steady, pulling a thread through Jerome's dead white skin, to close the massive wound. But he was as tense as everyone else. Ready to move the instant that Nicolò did —if he did.

Mircea wanted to have Horatiu take Dorina back upstairs, but he was afraid. Of sending her off with a human as her only guard. Of having her out of his sight. Of giving his "friends" a head start towards her. It was why she was by the wall, and Mircea was on the floor in front of her, with the implication clear: you will have to go through me.

So far, Nicolò hadn't. But his large hands were clenched, and his face was as frightening as Mircea had ever seen it. "Dhampir," he breathed again, and there was enough hate in it to still Mircea's hand.

"Child," another voice countered, and Marsilia came forward.

Mircea had almost forgotten about her, so intent had he been on Nicolò. But he was swiftly reminded when she moved to Dorina's side in the time it took him to blink. And smiled when he flinched.

And then transferred the expression to Dorina, who was looking up at her calmly. "That's a pretty picture," Marsilia said, squatting on the boards beside her.

Dorina wasn't particularly tall for her age; if anything, the opposite was true. But Marsilia was a tiny thing. And with her hair half down and most of her makeup lost to the storm that had broken out on the way here, they almost looked like sisters.

But they weren't, which was what had Mircea's back tensing and his leg muscles ready to spring.

Marsilia shot him a look that he couldn't exactly read, and turned her attention back to the paper Dory held.

Mircea bought the rough sheets from one of the local candy sellers, who used them to wrap around the sugary treats that Dorina loved so much. It was thin and worthless for anything you'd like to keep, but it served Mircea as a way to sketch out paintings before he committed them to expensive canvas. It was also one of the ways Horatiu used to keep Dory at home rather than running about the city on her own.

Eluding his half blind tutor wasn't much of a challenge for someone who had practically raised herself, since Mircea hadn't known she existed until a little over a year ago. And no one else in Venice had known it at all, after he brought her back from his travels, for the very obvious reason now staring him in the face. Well, they know it now, he thought, looking from Nicolò to his mistress, and wondering what he was going to do, because he couldn't take them both.

"Is that home?" Marsilia asked, kicking off the fashionable chopines she wore, and settling down into a more comfortable, cross-legged position.

"Mmm," Dorina looked at the paper thoughtfully. And

then added a few swipes of charcoal that somehow managed to convey the idea of a thick forest beyond the thatch-roofed cottage she'd already finished.

"It's very pretty," Marsilia repeated. "You're very talented."

Dorina shook her head. "Mircea," she said, nodding at the canvases stacked against the walls.

Horatiu had puttered about, muttering things, and reassembled them behind the table and easel that took up a good third of the catch-all room they mostly lived in. The bedrooms upstairs were dark and cramped, and the tiny kitchen was most definitely Horatiu's domain. Leaving this as the one place available for family activities.

Mircea had never wished so much that he'd somehow managed to afford a larger house, one like where he'd grown up, with servants and high, stone walls between danger and the people he loved.

Not that it had ever helped.

"Yes, he's full of surprises," Marsilia said mildly, thumbing through the canvases. "Ah." She pulled one free of the stack and regarded it with apparent pleasure. Mircea felt his hand tighten.

"Is this your mother?" Marsilia asked Dory, as Jerome made a small sound.

Mircea looked down to see that he'd pulled the cord too tight, threatening the evenness of his stitch work. And the integrity of his friend's flesh. "Almost done now," he reassured Jerome, who looked up at him with dazed eyes.

"Mmm." Dory said again. She was usually a chatterbox, but there were times, like tonight, when she almost seemed to have a separate personality. One who rarely spoke, but always watched, her dark eyes missing nothing.

"She's lovely," Marsilia decided, regarding the features of his now deceased wife, who Mircea had painted lying in a field of flowers, laughing and out of breath from the chase that had finally ended with him catching her.

It wasn't at all like the formal portraits he occasionally did for whatever patrons he could scrape up, or the even more stylized Madonnas he sold to a shopkeeper who always needed more to satisfy the pilgrims crowding the city like clockwork, for the circuit of festivals Venice's calendar boasted every year. Even with those, he was accused of adding things nobody wanted—curls that escaped from under the Virgin's coif, or a mended tear in her gown, or a too-mischievous grin on the face of the saintly child.

Mircea didn't know any saintly children, and he prized his daughter's rare smiles, so he'd painted the Christ child the same way. Like he'd painted his long-lost wife as he remembered her, which had been anything but stiff and stylized. Like that day, when she'd led him a merry chase.

It hadn't helped that she knew those woods far better than he, although he hadn't worried. He was bigger and stronger, his muscles honed by combat training, including fighting in full armor. He told himself that she'd tire long before him.

Only she hadn't. And she'd been fast, like quicksilver. He still suspected that she'd let him win, pausing on top of the flower-studded hill to allow him to locate her, and then fleeing down the other side.

But not quite fast enough.

"You look like her," Marsilia said, twisting the knife in Mircea's gut. She tilted Dorina's chin up. "You'll be a beauty someday. I know about these things."

"Marsilia—" Mircea began, his voice rough, only to be cut off by an explosion from Nicolò.

"She is dhampir. Why do you play games? You know what has to be done!"

"Do I?" Marsilia combed fingers through Dory's snarled hair, separating it into more manageable strands. "Why do I?"

"Children grow up!"

Marsilia began to braid Dory's hair. "Most do," she agreed.

"This isn't about her," Nicolò said, low and forceful. "This isn't about Sophia."

"No, it couldn't be, could it?" Marsilia asked mildly.

Dorina looked up at her, and Marsilia smiled. "I had a little girl once. She looked much like you. She would have been a beauty, too."

"Lia," Nicolò's voice cracked, with some emotion Mircea couldn't name.

"But I had her too young, you see? Far too young," Marsilia continued. "My body wasn't ready yet, and afterward, I found I couldn't have any more children. But that was all right. I had her."

"But she died," Dorina said calmly. She was watching Marsilia with an intensity that belied the non-expression on her face.

"Yes," Marsilia agreed. "A master vampire wanted to add me to his stable, but I didn't want to go. I had a daughter to care for, you see, and I worried about what would happen to her if I wasn't there to protect her."

"Lia," Nicolò said, his voice harsh. "This isn't the same thing."

"He killed her," Dorina guessed, sending a sharp pain through Mircea. Because of course he had. And, of course, Dorina knew it. Sometimes Mircea thought she understood this new world better than he ever would, having been born as part of it. It would always be a little alien to him, no matter how long he lived. But to her, it simply was.

To her, it was home.

"Of course he did," Marsilia agreed. "I cried for months; years, really. I still cry now, sometimes. For the girl she was, for the woman she might have been."

"Lia," Nicolò said, and she looked up, having finished a shining braid over Dorina's shoulder.

"I think we're done here," she said, rising with that same too-lithe movement. "Jerome needs time to rest and heal."

"You can't just expect us to—"

"We're done here," Marsilia said, her sweet voice a sudden crack, like the lash of a whip. "Do you understand?"

Her eyes swept the room, and her other vampires quickly nodded acquiescence, one even taking a knee. All except for

Nicolò. "She will grow up! One day, she may rip your throat out!"

Marsilia looked down at Dorina. "Will you?"

Dorina looked up at her. For a long, agonizing moment, she said nothing, just held Marsilia's dark gaze. And then, slowly, she shook her head.

Mircea thought about passing out.

"You see?" Marsilia asked Nicolò with a pretty smile. He did not smile back.

"Think it through! You can't mean to—"

He broke off when she grabbed him, lightning fast, to the point that Mircea's eyes never even registered the movement. One moment, the huge vampire was looming over their small family, and the next, he was bent almost double, his shirt in the fist of a very unhappy master.

"I will not become the thing who made me," Marsilia hissed. "I will not kill an innocent. And neither will you. Or that girl won't be the one ripping out your throat!"

There wasn't a lot of discussion after that.

CHAPTER FOUR

Present day, Dory
A messy kitchen in upstate New York

Somebody threw a glass of water in my face.

I sat up, sputtering, to find a curly-haired bastard leaning over me. "Feel better?"

The features belonging to Kit Marlowe, the senate's chief spy and resident asshole, slowly swam into view. The earring he always wore in one ear, like a goddamned pirate, winked cheekily at me. But at least today it was paired with a relatively normal slacks-and-dress-shirt combo, instead of something out of community theatre, and his dark hair and retro goatee looked like they might have been trimmed in the last week or three.

He looked almost respectable, not that it helped.

"Bite me," I slurred, the crashing sound of the ocean still in my ears.

"One day," Marlowe promised, and stood back up.

The kitchen was more crowded than before I took my second trip to Lala Land. There were a bunch of sheepish-looking servants who had gotten to the party too late, some vamps I assumed to be Marlowe's, since they had that same I-smell-something-nasty expression when they looked at me, and Gunther, with his arm all bandaged up. And appearing his usual self, except for the concern in those blue eyes.

"You okay?" he asked me.

"Need a beer," I croaked, and had a longneck tossed my way.

I almost didn't catch it, which, with dhampir reflexes, said everything about how out of it I still was. But I managed to snare it at the last second, and to get a thumb under the top, popping it open and chugging half before I looked up to see Gunther shaking his head. "What?"

"Just wishing I had thumbs of steel."

"It's a package deal," I told him dryly. Because I doubted he'd like the rest of the features.

I tried to get up, found it to be more of a challenge than usual, and decided fuck it. I stayed where I was and drank beer. And lowered the drained bottle to find Kit on his haunches in front of me, glaring.

"*Are* you all right?" he demanded, in a voice that made it clear that my well-being was not the point.

"And you care because?"

"I have a job for you, and you're going to want it. Question is, can you handle it?"

"Ask me after another beer."

Nobody gave me another beer. Marlowe stood up with an angry cat sound, and Gunther was occupied trying to calm down the still freaked-out chef. I'd have gone and gotten it myself, but someone was in the way.

Make that two someones.

"No, no. Gently," Radu admonished the pitiful thing sprawled on the floor of the kitchen.

She had tear-streaked makeup, a food-splashed body, and matted brown hair liberally dusted with frost. Because I guess we'd trapped the babies in the freezer, and it looked like it was a good one. Her eyes were red from crying, her mouth was open and panting, but her gaze never wavered from the single finger Radu was holding up.

It was bleeding slightly, a tiny dot of almost black, the color only centuries of power can produce. I'd seen it bring Mircea, Radu's brother and my father, back from the brink of death recently, and just the sight seemed to have absolutely mesmerized the baby vamp. She followed the digit with a little swaying motion of her head as Radu waggled it at her admonishingly. And then finally let her taste.

"Gently," he repeated, but there was no need. As soon as the bloody thing touched her tongue, her face relaxed into a cross between desperate-junkie-getting-a-fix and devotee-seeing-the-face-of-god. It was more than a little disturbing. I looked away, only to hear Radu say, "No, no. Not too much, dear. Else we'll pull you away from your Sire, and Misha wouldn't like that, now would he?"

"Misha?" I repeated, remembering what the chef had said. "Radu, what is going on? Why are we taking care of another family's babies?"

"Ask him," Radu said darkly, glancing at Marlowe.

"They're to be used as functionaries at court," Marlowe said curtly. "But there aren't enough beds for them, so the overflow had to go somewhere."

I frowned. The court part made sense. Louis-Cesare, in what I regarded as a bad move, had decided to locate his new court all of twenty minutes from the one owned by the consul, the powerful leader of the North American Vampire Senate. That would have been bad enough, since it left him handy for whatever errand she'd thought up this time, but it was especially so at the moment. Because her creepy-looking house was acting as a sort of court of courts for the droves of masters pouring in to discuss the war.

We were currently fighting a coalition of fey, rogue vampires, and dark mages, which would have sounded like a bad movie of the week if they hadn't recently masterminded an attack that had resulted in a whole lot of deaths on our side. They'd suffered more, but I doubted that was much comfort to the families of the fallen. Especially since some of those families had been together for hundreds of years.

Masters were assembling from literally everywhere to decide on a response, and I guess they'd needed somewhere to rest up in between the policy making, back-biting, and general intrigue. So it made sense that the consul's place was packed. And that the lowly babies would be kicked out to find lodgings elsewhere.

Or it would have, except that they shouldn't have been there at all.

Baby vamps were useless for anywhere from two months to two years after the Change, and sometimes longer. Not only couldn't they see properly, but they also couldn't control anything else about their new bodies either. Like trying to move a little faster and accidentally plowing through a wall. Or attempting to open a jar and shattering it into pieces. Or going into a panic about a fire ten miles away.

Not surprisingly, nobody took them anywhere. Most people didn't even let them out of the house. And now the consul was putting them to work?

"Functionaries?" I repeated, not bothering to keep the disbelief out of my voice.

"People to answer phones, type things, run errands." Marlowe waved it away.

"I know what the word means! But why not just hire some more humans? They're better in daylight anyway, not to mention—"

"She doesn't trust humans."

"Some mid-level vamps, then."

"They're busy."

"Doing what?"

"None of your business!"

I stared at him, my vision pulsing in and out enough that it looked like he was constantly lunging at me. Lunge, retreat, lunge retreat. That was a problem, since I had been known to invoke incandescent rage in Marlowe before.

So how was I supposed to know when he really lost it?

I leaned my head back against a cabinet and shut my eyes, since they weren't helping. "Fine, don't tell me."

"I hadn't planned to."

"Then why are you here?"

"I am beginning to wonder that myself."

He was glaring again. I couldn't see him, but I could hear it in his voice. Could feel it in the dhampir part of me that wanted to go for his throat. But not as badly as usual.

Maybe it had a headache, too.

Someone snarled, and I opened my eyes to see that Bitey had been let out.

He was faintly blue, and beads of ice had formed in the sweat in his hair. They made little clacking sounds when he moved his head, looking wildly about. And then howling, a sound of mingled rage and hunger, as he dove for Radu's messy finger.

Only to be stopped mid-pounce by a flood of power that prickled over my skin and raised the hair on the back of my neck. It made several of Marlowe's guys tense up and stare around, as if wondering where it was coming from. Because, somehow, everybody always forgot that Radu was a second-level master.

The camouflage, I had to admit, was compelling.

I sighed and relaxed back against the cabinets instead of rescuing my uncle, who clearly didn't need it. But the flood of power didn't have the same effect on the baby. He fought and thrashed and howled, flailing his arms and gnashing his teeth, despite the fact that he wasn't going anywhere.

The frown on 'Du's handsome face became a bit more pronounced.

"If you aren't good, you won't get any at all," Du rebuked him. "And if you're not calmed down by me, we can't trust you with one of the donors, now can we?"

The baby roared.

"He ees too far gone; he doesn't understand," the chef said, from across the kitchen. "And must zees be done 'ere? I 'ave *le diner* to consider."

Radu didn't move, or so much as look up. But Gunther moved to steer the unhappy chef away. "I merely said zat I cannot cook under zese conditions!" the vamp told him.

Gunther patted his shoulder. "It's okay. We'll get take-out."

"Take-out? *Take-out*, in my kit—"

The door shut.

"Verrell might be right," I said, eyeing Bitey. "He looks a little . . . upset."

"No, he understands," Radu said, watching the furious thing still pawing the air.

Until the finger moved a little closer, and Bitey's mouth suddenly went slack.

"You feel it, don't you?" Radu asked, his voice velvet. "Who we are, what you are now, in blood and flesh and bone. Not an animal to act so, to lash out as the humans do. And not a monster, as they so often call us. But more than you have ever been. A fusion of flesh and spirit, a masterpiece of nature; a man still, but one perfected, with the old weaknesses left behind, and an infinity of promise ahead. You *feel* it, don't you?"

It looked like he felt something. I didn't know if it was because of Radu's power or his words, but Bitey was no longer living up to his name. And he wasn't looking at the finger, despite the fact that it was slowly being offered now. His eyes were on 'Du, wide and shocked. Whose own eyes were glowing faintly as he pressed the blood to the man's lips, smearing it on his flesh like a pagan priest initiating an acolyte.

"You're creeping me out, 'Du," I muttered, while servants came forward to lead the dazed-looking vamp away.

"Oh, that's rich, coming from you," Radu said, and rose from the filthy kitchen floor, gazing with disapproval at his ripped hose and stained clothing. "Tomato sauce. It never comes out of satin," he informed me, nonetheless patting at it with a cloth.

"Coming from me? What does that mean?"

A single eyebrow raised. He knew how much I hated that. "Did you or did you not round up all the babies in the place and corral them in your closet?"

"What?" I stared at him. "Why on earth would I do that?"

"Well, I don't know." It was peevish. "That's what I planned to ask you. But every time they tried to leave, or anyone tried to go in and get them, you snarled at them—"

"I don't snarl."

"You snarl quite convincingly. It's terrifying. And for such a pretty girl." Radu reached down to tilt my face up. "They are going to love you in Paris. If you don't snarl at them, that is."

And, just like that, another wave of disorientation hit and hit hard. I saw a tiny pixie of a vampire again, felt her gentle touch on my skin, heard the deceptively sweet voice echo in my head: "You'll be a beauty someday. I know about these things…"

I put my head on my knees and just breathed for a moment.

I supposed it was only fair that I was getting flashbacks, even if they weren't mine, to old Venice, since that's where my problems had mostly started. Before then, I'd been a fairly normal half-human, half-bloodsucking fiend—okay, so normal had never really described me. But I'd been closer, like one whole mind closer, until Mircea had decided to split it. And had somehow created two brains out of one, isolating the human me from the vampire version, which he claimed was necessary to save my life.

And maybe it had been. Maybe the vampire me really had been threatening to swamp my far less powerful human half, resulting in the madness dhampirs were famous for. I didn't know. Because the process had wiped human-me's mind, to the point that I didn't remember jack about the family's time in Venice.

Or about a lot of other things, since Dorina, my vamp version, had the memories from all the times she'd been in control.

That had always been a gut punch, since it often resulted in me waking up surrounded by the bodies she'd massacred after deciding that I was in over my head and taking charge. It had been my body who'd killed those people, but not my brain giving the okay—not all of it, anyway—resulting in some serious soul-searching. And a fair amount of PTSD from having a possibly evil doppelganger who could emerge whenever she chose, especially if I lost my temper and therefore my mental control.

And so it had gone, me hulking out for the last five centuries or so, because Mircea had decided that that was the best way to contain my mental problems. Only they weren't anymore. Contained, that is, because the barrier he'd built in my cranium had failed in a spectacular way recently, leaving Dorina and me in intermittent communication for the first time. Which she had mostly been using to send me crazy memories whenever I passed out.

Because my other half was apparently a psycho.

"We haven't established that she's going anywhere yet," Marlowe's pissy voice said, cutting through the mental din.

"Of course she's going," 'Du said. "Who else could track my son half so well?"

"Track . . . what?" I raised my head, the pounding migraine suddenly less important than that careless, half-heard phrase.

"Who, dear."

"What?"

"Track who, not what. We're not talking about some kind of wild beast, after all."

"I—what?"

"You keep saying that. Stop saying that."

I felt my world tilting into the bizarre, which was not unusual when talking to my batty uncle. As the younger brother of Mircea Basarab, first-level master, senate member, and all-around bad dude to cross, Radu had spent entirely too many years being able to say whatever he wanted to whoever he chose. It had gotten to the point that, some days, he didn't bother to make any damned sense at all.

Like now, for instance.

"Radu—" I began grimly.

"He's talking about Louis-Cesare. He's disappeared," Marlowe cut in.

"What do you mean, disappeared?" I demanded.

"It's probably nothing," Radu said, fussing over the latest baby. "You know how Louis-Cesare is."

And, yes, yes I did. Proud to the point of arrogance, self-confident to the point of recklessness, a powerful prima donna who was almost as strong as he thought he was, yet also strangely vulnerable because of an outdated sense of noblesse oblige and a not very well hidden bleeding heart. If he hadn't been such a formidable opponent, he'd have been dead years ago. As it was, he frequently gave me aneurysms without even trying.

"*Is* it nothing?" I asked Marlowe, who had crouched in front of me again, looking grim.

"No."

"Tell me."

Dark brown eyes met mine, shrewd and assessing. "Are you up to this?"

"Yes! And I need to—"

A hand like a striking snake grabbed my arm. "Don't lie to me," he growled. "I have to put someone on this, and for a variety of reasons, you were first on the list. But then I find you like this," he gestured at the blood and ice-cream-stained baby doll, "and learn that you've been out of your head for the best part of two days! I would prefer to keep this low-key, but if I have to risk an international incident—"

"An international incident?" I frowned. "Over a missing master?"

"No." Marlowe's throat worked, and his eyes looked like they were trying to bore a hole into my head. But he finally came out with it. "Over a missing consul. Anthony hasn't been heard from in a week, leading us to send Louis-Cesare to locate him. And now we've lost contact with him, too."

CHAPTER FIVE

1457, Mircea
Still at the wart, Venice, Italy

Mircea rolled over and fell out of bed. He lay there for a moment, because that hadn't been normal even when he was human, and it certainly wasn't now. One of the few advantages of his new state was a fine sense of balance, which ensured that he didn't usually fall on his face.

Of course, he didn't usually have a master vamp in his bed, either.

He regarded Jerome's sprawled form, which covered all but perhaps a fifth of the narrow bed, with annoyance. And then he got up to check on his friend. His color was still bad, but that was likely because he wasn't expending power to make it otherwise. And his incessant snoring, which had kept Mircea up half the day, seemed to indicate that some resting was going on. Mircea threw the bedcover, which had ended up on the floor along with him, back over Jerome and headed downstairs.

He paused on the landing to check on Dorina. The tiny room across from his had been Horatiu's, until he paid a couple of muscle-bound types to drag home a box bed he'd found in one of the city's numerous pawn shops. It was essentially a cabinet with a bed in it that he'd stuck in one end of the kitchen, near the fire, because "old bones don't like the cold as well as young ones do." Or dead ones, Mircea had thought, and helped him put the pieces together.

As a result, when Dorina arrived, the only other bedroom in the little house had become hers. She'd since covered it with drawings of Venice and its people, along with memories of home. Leaving Mircea looking at fields and streams and tall, conical hay bales; at gnarled old women in gypsy garb, wrists spangled with bracelets; at ramshackle wagons covered with carvings; and at a crowd of dirty, dancing feet. Here he was, splattered with paint and frowning at a canvas; there was Horatiu, peering myopically at a pot over the fire, his long nose almost touching the soup; and a little above that, a couple of the neighbor's kids were playing dice in the street.

There was her mother, weaving in a corner of her small house, a ray of sunlight in her hair.

Mircea pulled the small scrap off the wall and held it up. There was no window in the hall, but vampire eyes didn't need one, not with moonbeams streaming into the landing from a dozen cracks in the boards. It was enough to show him what he'd expected: this wasn't an image he knew.

It wasn't one of the sketches he'd made, ostensibly to show Dorina her mother's face, but in reality so he wouldn't forget it himself. It had been more than a decade since he'd seen Elena; a decade since he'd left her, standing in the door of her house, tears of anger and anguish streaming down her face; a decade since he'd told himself that he was doing the right thing, and getting away before the madness of his new condition caused him to hurt or kill her.

A decade, and he was only realizing now that he'd probably hurt her far more by leaving than he ever would have by the reverse.

He'd gone back, after some of the madness lifted, and he'd discovered that he was still a man, simply a changed one. The idea had been to give her the choice he'd previously denied her, whether to stay with him as he was, or for them to have a proper farewell. But what he'd found were rumors of her horrific death, a murderous bastard of a brother, and a daughter he'd never even known he had.

There had been no question about taking Dorina back with him, no question that she deserved whatever advantages he could give her, poor though they might be. It had never occurred to him that someone might object. She was his daughter; of course he would help her.

But she was dhampir, too, conceived in the narrow window between the laying of the curse that had upended his life, and the completion of it. It had only taken a few days, but it had been enough to engender a life that was neither one thing nor another. A life hated by his new tribe, and feared by his old. He had done this to her, had made sure she would never fit in with either group, and might well be hunted by both of them.

And he had no idea how to fix it.

He reached in the door to smooth her hair back from her forehead. Silky soft and abundant, so like her mother's. Her little nape, so vulnerable, like the slender arm that had fought its way free of the covers.

She barely stirred when he put it back underneath. Perhaps she knew it was him, or perhaps she was exactly as she appeared: a child, lost in dreams. Would she have roused at someone else's touch?

Would she have roused at Nicolò's?

Not that the vampire worried him so much anymore; Marsilia had him well in hand. But there would be others. A great many of them, in all likelihood, especially if the family stayed here. Or anywhere else in Venice.

The city had long been a refuge for people like him, for vampires cursed instead of made, with no master to protect them. Or for ones rejected by their masters, or made accidentally during a feeding that went wrong, or runaways that nobody cared enough about to pursue. There were a thousand stories behind the people who washed up here, in what had once been the only safe zone in the vampire world, a place where they wouldn't be hunted by others of their kind.

And who still did, in droves, despite the recent upheaval.

For the first time in two thousand years, there were new consuls in charge of Europe's vampires. That was apparently not unusual for the other senates, which Mircea occasionally heard rumors about. It sounded like they were constantly changing consuls, in bloody coups that people only whispered about, even this far away.

But that had not been true here. Not for millennia, time out of mind. Because Europe's consul hadn't just been a powerhouse, he'd been a monster, far older than all the rest. And one whom Mircea wasn't sure had been entirely vampire, and not something else altogether.

But he'd been taken down nonetheless, by two of his powerful, and possibly mad Children: Anthony, the boisterous, lecherous, brave, and flamboyant, one-time Master of Horse for Julius Caesar, and the woman who had been his lover for two millennia. The woman with whom he'd once dared to challenge the greatest empire the world had ever known.

She was called merely The Consul now, as if there weren't two of them. As if they weren't bound together in a duumvir-like situation such as had once been common in the human world, but was previously unknown in the vampire. Which had never before seen two people share power.

It was seeing it now.

And yet, when people spoke, it was always thus: Anthony and The Consul.

Mircea wondered if that rankled, wondered how long such an unusual situation could last. But that didn't matter to him, who barely qualified as part of their world. What did matter was the new consuls' emphasis on the rule of law over caprice. And that masters no longer had complete control over their Children's lives, to make, kill, or cast them aside at will.

The new laws had drastically reduced the number of masterless vampires being made; well, that and the fact that the worst offenders were at war with the new consuls, and didn't have time for such things these days. Several more free zones had also been set up, with safe passage between them, because many of the excluded had never managed to reach Venice. And the hounding of those who did, and who had previously been shaken down for all they were worth by the local guards, had been stopped. By any possible measure, things were vastly better than they had been.

Yet no master was still no master.

Mircea pulled the curtain over Dorina's door closed and started down the rickety stairs.

The problem was the patchwork of territories that powerful masters had spread across the land, which was still in effect. And which was likely to remain so, at least for the foreseeable future, since the consuls needed their vassals' help against the rebels opposing the change of power, and couldn't risk alienating them further. Leaving his kind with few options, unless they had a skill that a master might want.

But even if he was willing to put himself under someone else's power, something he'd avoided so far, and even assuming he found anyone interested in acquiring his services, what were the odds of them also accepting Dorina?

Marsilia was the exception, not the rule, and her compassion came from a pain others did not know. He couldn't expect to be so lucky again. Leaving him trapped in a city filled with creatures far stronger than he, every single one of whom thought his daughter was a monster who should be killed on sight.

"Now, now, none of that," Horatiu said, peering at him as he came into the kitchen. "We had enough trauma last night, I should think."

"Aren't you going to ask how Jerome is?" Mircea asked, sliding into a place at the tiny table.

Horatiu had somehow managed to wedge it between the box bed and the protrusion out over the sea that looked like a wart growing on a wart, but which served as a fireplace. It made the already small kitchen ridiculously cramped, but Horatiu had insisted. He might be serving one monster out of legend, might be tutoring another, might have left home and hearth behind to live in a city stuffed to the gills with even more of them. But he'd be damned if he'd eat on the floor like a peasant.

"He's a master, and he's still breathing," the old man

returned sardonically. "I know how he is."

He shoveled some leftover fish pie with figs into a bowl and poured them both some ale. Mircea couldn't taste it, of course; taste was yet another thing he'd lost to the Change, and which only returned for the lucky few who reached master status. And without a master of his own to draw power from, he was unlikely to ever be among their number. But he found the ritual soothing, nonetheless: sitting by a fire, drinking with a friend. Almost like the last ten years had never happened.

But they had. And with them had come responsibilities he'd never expected, and didn't know how to fulfill. Foremost among these was keeping his daughter safe.

"You're doing it again," Horatiu grumbled.

"How do you know what I'm doing?" Mircea asked. "You're not even looking at me."

"Don't have to look at you, do I?" Horatiu remained bent over his bowl, shoveling in food. "Known you since you were a boy. Always moody."

Mircea frowned some more, while his old tutor continued to inhale his meal. Horatiu had been around Dorina too long; he bolted his food these days, as if he was afraid that someone would take it away from him. And, knowing Venice, someone might, if Mircea wasn't around to protect him. Another welcome burden; another desperate fear. The old man might have been killed last night, and then what would Mircea have done?

Without his greatest friend.

"Keep that look on your face one more minute, and I'll hit ye with a spoon," Horatiu said, mopping up the juices from the pie with a stale end of bread.

Mircea sighed. "What do you think about France?"

Horatiu leaned back on his stool, finding the comfortable spot he'd worn into the old boards, and let out a belch.

"Was that cholic or commentary?" Mircea asked dryly.

"Bit of both. Demmed figs."

Mircea sighed some more. "I know what we decided. But this latest incident —"

"Changes nothing."

"I have friends in France, and Paris is a free zone now —"

"Aye. And how friendly d'you think they'd be, once they found out about the little princess?"

"She isn't a princess—"

"Her father was a prince. You up and married her mother, and commoner or no, that makes her—"

"I'm not a prince any longer."

"Don't interrupt," Horatiu said, scowling, as if he hadn't just done the same to Mircea three times in a row. "She's a princess, and that's that."

"She's a *dhampir*, and that's that," Mircea said, the fear gnawing at his gut raising his voice. "She can't stay here, surrounded by the very things that want to kill her!"

"And she'd be better off in France, surrounded by far more powerful types, who could sense her more easily?"

"We'd live in the countryside. And the ones here sensed her well enough, last night."

"Aye. Because she wanted them to."

Mircea narrowed his eyes.

"Don't give me that look," Horatiu said, and Mircea wondered again how a man who had grown progressively blind over the years, to the point that he regularly got lost trying to find their house, could still see the slightest sign of defiance in his old charge. It was uncanny.

"Then explain what you meant."

Horatiu shrugged. "Simple enough. You know how she is. Runs off whenever she pleases to play with those street children. I've told her repeatedly, they're not proper friends for one of her station, but does she mind?" He shot Mircea a look. "Reminds me of someone else I know."

"Having friends in low places can be useful," Mircea retorted. "As we just had demonstrated."

And not that they were any different, these days. They lived in a slum region of Venice, in a house that looked like it was about to slide into the sea. While he cheated at cards and tried to sell his art, in a town where every passing boatman fancied himself an artist. And half of them were better than him!

They barely kept their heads above water, yet Horatiu was worried about standards. Mircea was worried about survival. Standards could look after themselves.

"Useful for you," Horatiu retorted. "Not for Dorina."

"Did you have a point?"

"I already said: she runs off all the time, a fact I bemoaned —and continue to do so for the lack of propriety. But I no longer worry about her safety. Fair scared me to death, she did, the first few times. But then I started following her, y'see."

"Not really," Mircea said dryly. Because the only way Horatiu had managed to follow anyone, much less Dorina, was if she let him.

"I followed her," the old man said sternly. "Several times. And t'was always the same. We passed vampires here and there, can't swing a dead cat in this city without hitting one. But they never so much as flinched. They just didn't notice her."

"Well, they noticed her last night!"

"Because she wanted them to. She can hide or reveal her nature, or even project it, I reckon, considering how hard it hit 'em." He looked at Mircea narrowly, the vague eyes suddenly shrewd. "She takes after you in art. Did ye really think that was the only way?"

Mircea just sat there, slightly stunned. A ten-year-old dhampir was hard enough to keep track of. A ten-year-old dhampir with mental powers was frankly terrifying. And what about when she was older?

What the hell was he supposed to do when she was older?

And that assumed she even made it that far.

Mircea had a sudden, overwhelming desire to start banging his head against the table, and just not stop. Only, knowing how things worked now, he'd probably just break the table. And he'd never hear the end of that, since he didn't have the money to replace it.

Someone cleared a throat behind him, the noise loud

and unexpected. Even more so because—impossibly—he hadn't heard them approach. Which was why, a second later, the throat-clearer was against the wall with a knife to his neck.

"I should have scuffed a shoe?" Jerome asked, gray eyes wide.

Mircea stepped back, repressing a curse. And then said it anyway. "What were you thinking? You're hurt badly enough!"

"I'm sorry. I didn't mean to startle you." He glanced from Mircea to Horatiu, who was half out of his chair in alarm, and then back again. "Or to eavesdrop. But I couldn't help overhearing."

He could have probably done that from his room, with a master's ears, so Mircea didn't doubt it. He put the knife down. "It doesn't matter."

"I think it does. And I think . . . there may be a way we can help each other."

CHAPTER SIX

Present Day, Dory
Somewhere in the skies over the Atlantic

I stared at my bleary, bloodshot eyes in the tiny airplane mirror.

"Are you done?" I asked thickly, and got another horrible, upswelling surge for an answer.

Guess not.

Despite a life spanning way more centuries than I liked to remember, I didn't have a lot of experience with hangovers. Or with what came before them. My metabolism usually whisked anything I gave it out of my bloodstream before I had a chance to know it was there, which was great when drinking socially or deciding to eat a whole pie. But it was a bitch when you just wanted to drown your sorrows.

Or when you really, really needed to.

I tried to talk my stomach into not losing the one concoction that could put me on my ass. Or, in this case, on a toilet lid while hanging over a sink, trying to keep down what really wanted to come back up. And the bitch of it was, the damned stuff wasn't even helping.

Or maybe it was, and I just couldn't tell, because *God*.

"Dory? Are you all right in there?" Radu's voice drifted through the plane's lightweight door.

I tried to answer, and immediately regretted it.

"Dory?"

My stomach was not cooperating with my vocal cords right now, and I really wanted Radu to go sit back down. The stewardess apparently did, too, because she was trying to get the drink cart past. I could hear her telling him to please resume his seat, something that had no effect because 'Du was used to hearing only what he wanted to, even from people with a lot more clout than a pretty girl in the friendly skies.

Which were about to get a lot less friendly, because Marlowe had just joined the party.

"What's wrong with her?" I heard him demand, somewhere back in the world of the living.

"I don't know. She isn't answering."

A sharp knuckle rapped imperiously on the door, while I wished for a trashcan or possibly to die.

"Dorina! What is wrong with you?"

The fact that I'm thirty-five thousand feet in the air with three bottles of fey wine in me, I didn't say, because I was busy.

Two and a half now, I thought, and ran some water in the sink, because it was getting ripe in here.

"I think she's almost done," Radu said, sounding relieved. And then annoyed. "Young woman, cease banging my ankles with that infernal contraption immediately."

"My apologies, sir," came the least sincere reply ever. "But it's time for drinks service."

Drinks, I thought.

Oh, *God.*

"She isn't done, she's puking it all up, and we don't have any more," Marlowe said, rattling the door. "Let me in!"

It was softly spoken, because we weren't in one of the senate jets, or the smaller, Saudi-prince-on-a-budget version that Mircea owned. Those were busy ferrying people to whatever confab the consul was currently holding about the war. And, as the newly elected leader of the vampire world, her word was law, even when that word required—gasp—flying coach.

So that was where we were, three stooges in the cheap seats, because that had been the only thing left on exactly zero notice. Which would have been fine, since I wasn't used to private jets anyway, and the only other alternative, ley line travel, was a mile-a-second roller coaster through rivers of pure power. Which, if your shield wobbled even for an instant, could incinerate you before you could scream.

On the whole, the cheap seats had sounded fine.

Until I found out what Marlowe had planned for in-flight entertainment.

"Damn it! Open this door!"

He was getting louder, not that it mattered, since Radu was already berating the stewardess loudly enough to alert the whole plane. If they kept this up, the pilot was going to turn around and take us back to JFK, and the only thing I could think of worse than being piss drunk and hungover at the same time was doing it at JFK. Which, as airports go, stands for Just Fucking Kill me already and—

Somebody's fist punched through the door.

Judging by the huge ruby on one finger, it was Marlowe's. Not surprising, since the arrogant prick wasn't used to waiting— or to being flipped off, considering the expression in the eye that appeared in the newly made hole. A second later, the hand was back, the latch was flicked, and I had company.

A lot of company, because Radu was muscling in, too, possibly to get out of the way of the cart. Only that wasn't helping, because the stewardess—now alarmed about a broken door and a possible *ménage a trois* in the Mile High Club—was pulling on 'Du. Who was flapping back at her ineffectually with those long, pale hands of his, because he had the usual vamp fear of breaking the fragile humans. Which meant he was basically wrestling with the equivalent of a spun glass statue and wasn't getting anywhere.

Until he turned to try to break her hold and ended up pushing her inside and shoving the door closed behind them.

Leaving me scrunched into a corner with Marlowe, virtually nose to nose.

His wrinkled.

"How much did you lose?" he demanded, with exactly zero sympathy.

"Fuck you," I whispered, as my stomach rumbled threateningly.

And then did it louder when Radu elbowed me in it. It seemed that the stewardess had decided we were some sort of terrorist group, or possibly mad, and was defending her flight by beating the hell out of 'Du. And screeching, at least until Marlowe snapped a "Go to sleep!" in her direction.

Radu blinked at him over top of the woman's head, as she abruptly slumped in his arms. "You said we couldn't do that."

"I said *you* couldn't, and answer me!"

I guess that last was aimed at me, although he was still glaring at 'Du. Who was glaring right back, and imperious former sort-of-kings do it pretty well. Radu was one of the only people I knew who wouldn't be intimidated by an angry chief spy.

Well, and the gal about to hurl all over him.

"Answer me, and stop that!" Marlowe said, which would have been confusing except that I'd just started poking him in the stomach. Hard. Which was better than what was about to happen if he didn't get out of the way.

"Before you hork it all up, did you get anything?" he demanded, shaking me.

"Not done horking," I said indistinctly, and saw his eyes widen.

A split second later, I was bent over the sink, doing a repeat performance, while Radu berated Marlowe. But not about me. Radu has his own form of kindness, even compassion, at times. But from his perspective, I was already taking care of my problem, while he still had his.

"You mean to tell me we could have just—why are we subjecting ourselves to this?" Radu demanded, gesturing around at the completely unacceptable accommodations over the top of the woman's thick bun. It was starting to come down now, and her lipstick had smeared all over the mostly normal summer suit that Marlowe's men had stuffed him into, which already had him in a mood. And that was before we ended up in steerage, as he determinedly kept calling it.

"We have a treaty with the mages—"

"As if anybody pays attention to that old thing!"

"The senate pays attention," Marlowe snapped. "We're the ones bound to enforce it!"

"Yes, when it suits you—"

"Which it does when the only advantage to breaking it is to your overweening pride!"

"Over—" Radu's eyes widened, and his back straightened, causing the unconscious woman to flop over to the other side. "Why you insufferable—"

"Peasant? Yes, yes, I was actually—or damned close to it—"

Someone new started banging on the door.

"Why am I not surprised?" Radu said, managing to pop an imperious eyebrow despite the circumstances. "The complete lack of any kind of breeding—"

"My kind were bred to survive. Something you know very little about!" Marlowe snarled and slammed open the door.

Radu looked both confused and outraged by that, although the latter might have been because of the steward who had just been jerked inside and passed over. Leaving him draped with unconscious humans he was struggling to see past. "I still seem to be here!" he nonetheless managed to point out.

"Yes! Thanks to your—" Marlowe caught himself, but not in time. He'd been on edge all day, maybe because he had two high-level missing persons, a couple of assistants he didn't trust at all, and a war to fight. The latter of which would become increasingly difficult if our new allies found out that we couldn't even corral our own people. And they would find out, despite Marlowe's attempts at remaining incognito by using human transport, and pretty damned fast, too.

Because we weren't the only senate to have a spymaster.

"Thanks to my what?" Radu asked, sounding ominous.

And then somebody knocked on the door again.

"Oh, for—go to sleep!" Marlowe said forcefully enough that I felt the suggestion hit me on its way to knock out the latest sweet young thing in the doorway.

"You first," she said, and slipped inside, shutting the door. Leaving her and Marlowe staring at each other over my backside, while I struggled to throw off the unintended suggestion.

And then wondered why I bothered, because a nap sounded really good right now.

"Who the hell are you?" Marlowe demanded, looking her up and down. She had on a stewardess outfit, a neat blue and white number that complemented a trim figure and a blond updo, but obviously wasn't one based on the fact that she hadn't hit the floor yet.

And those shoes, I thought groggily. No human would wear four-inch heels in a job like hers. It was always the little things that gave it away. Not that I cared how many vamps they stuffed in here.

I have had it with these motherfucking vamps on this motherfucking plane, I thought suddenly, and giggled.

"What is wrong with you?" Marlowe demanded.

"Do we get those little pillows in tourist class?" I asked the girl, ignoring him.

Her lips twitched. "I think that could be arranged."

"Oh, good." I looked around, but didn't see one. But Marlowe's chest proved to be surprisingly comfortable.

For about five seconds.

"Wake the hell up!" he told me, which didn't help, because most of my sleepiness was due to too much booze, rather than a vamp suggestion.

But two other people's weren't.

And, for the record, six people in a tourist class loo is too damned many, especially when two of them are fairly hysterical.

Make that three, I thought, as 'Du went down, being trampled by stewardess #1's sensible shoes.

"It's all right, Caroline," the blonde said, catching the other woman's eyes. "Go back to sleep. I'll deal with this."

"Deal with it how?" Marlowe asked. "Who are you?"

"You, too, Greg," she added, because her male counterpart

had woken up and already had a fist halfway to Marlowe's face.

"She's European consular security," I said, sitting on the side of the sink and pulling my knees up, because Radu was still flailing around on the floor.

"How did you know?" she asked, curious and a little wary. "Can you read my mind?"

"Not in the skill set."

"That's not what I hear."

"And where would you hear anything?" Marlowe demanded.

"We have sources, same as you." The woman tilted her head at me. "If you don't carry your father's gift, how did you know?"

I sighed and thought longingly about that pillow. "You're a vamp in disguise, following us—"

"Which I could be doing for any number of reasons."

"—and you've no aura." I swatted groggily at the air, where the power that envelops all vamps was sparking and hissing, filling the cramped space with what looked like colorful fog. Two clouds of it, because Marlowe and Radu's powers were duking it out. But hers wasn't. As far as I could see, and with my new, Dorina-enhanced vision, I could see a lot, it just wasn't there at all.

"Anybody with that kind of talent is picked up by special forces early," I added. "And since Marlowe doesn't know you, and considering why we're here—"

"That's enough!" he told me, before I gave the game away.

Like we had any game.

"I know why you're here," she said, looking from Marlowe to me and then to Radu, who had regained his dignity and was now sitting primly on the john. Her forehead wrinkled. "At least, I think I do. Radu is Louis-Cesare's Sire; if anyone can find him, it should be him. And Lord Marlowe is the consul's chief of intelligence. Anthony is her foremost ally, and she is planning strategy for the war; of course, she needs him back. But you... If you don't have your father's gift, what can you do?"

"Tell her nothing!" Marlowe said, staring at her. He hadn't seemed to notice the lack of aura until I pointed it out, but now that he had, he was obviously unhappy about it. Maybe because, without one, he couldn't tell what family she belonged to, and it was making him twitchy.

"She didn't have to announce herself," I said, watching his hands. Which were kind of looking like they'd appreciate being wrapped around someone's neck. I'd seen Marlowe angry plenty of times—it was practically his default around me—but today was something new. Today was something special.

And that probably wasn't good.

That probably meant he hadn't leveled with us.

I started wondering exactly how this could get worse while he and the girl glared at each other. "Check my bona fides," she told him tersely. "I work directly under Senator Heinrich. Ask him if you—" she broke off, because Marlowe had just gone into that creepy, slack-faced mode masters use when communicating mentally. She glanced at me, looking half exasperated and half freaked out that this was what we called a rescue team.

But it was either that, or risk alerting everyone to the consul's inability to keep up with her allies right when she needed to look strong. Vamps had a tendency to fight like cats— powerful, deadly, short-tempered cats—and most of them were pissed that she'd somehow ended up as their leader anyway. Not that it was supposed to last for long; the unprecedented alliance of the world's vampire senates was only for the duration of the war, and only because they'd finally found something scarier than they were. Namely, a bunch of ancient gods who had decided to come back from outer space, or wherever the hell they'd been hanging out since the *Iliad*, and stomp all our asses.

So we suddenly had this alliance to, you know, stop that. Only everybody in it pretty much hated everybody else, and the consul was left trying to herd not only cats, but angry cats, and if I hadn't disliked her so much, I might have felt a vague twinge of sympathy. As it was, I was forced into cheering her on, simply because I didn't want to die along with the rest of humanity. And that would have meant solving this little mystery pdq, even if Louis-Cesare, my boyfriend of the terrible taste, wasn't involved.

He wasn't dead; I'd know if he was dead. But he was obviously in trouble, because I'd practically drowned myself in the substance that helped me access Dorina's mental gifts—she got all the fun stuff from dear old Dad—but not a peep. And the thought of what that might mean was making me sick even without the booze.

"Can you help?" the female vamp asked me, as Marlowe's face started contorting with the expressions he was using in his chat with his European counterpart. Vamps usually masked that sort of thing because silent communication doesn't help much if you give an expressive play-by-play of the process. But it kind of looked like he was past caring.

"I don't know," I told her honestly. "Sometimes, Louis-Cesare and I seem to have a sort of connection, but it isn't working right now."

"It isn't working with Anthony, either," she said, biting her lip. "We've been on this for over a week, and nothing."

"Well, there's always the old-fashioned way. Where were the two of them seen last?"

"The same place. But it's... difficult... to get in there."

"Difficult to get in where?" I asked, wondering what on earth could stymie even a vampire senate's resources.

She told me.

And, suddenly, Radu popped up, looking surprisingly perky for someone who had recently been stomped on.

"Oh, love, that's not impossible at all. I already have us an appointment!"

CHAPTER SEVEN

1457, Mircea
A creepy alleyway in Venice, Italy

I did have bodyguards," Jerome said, as they made their way through a ridiculously narrow alley. "Or assistants, anyway."

"It doesn't appear to have helped," Mircea pointed out, glancing behind him.

"We were ambushed," Jerome said savagely. "We'd barely disembarked before they grabbed us!"

Mircea was suddenly wishing he hadn't asked for details, at least not here. The little path that was almost brushing his shoulders on either side was made even more confining by the second and third stories of houses that had been pushed out over it. They were designed to gain the neighbors a little extra living space, but they also blocked out much of the sky, turning the alley into more of a tunnel than a street. One with few options for escape were things to go wrong.

And on this street, things frequently did.

This wasn't the vamp part of Venice. This was the mage part, and it had always made Mircea's skin crawl. He'd heard that some of his kind, the older ones especially, liked little confined places. To the point that they often made their courts underground, where the sun couldn't penetrate and where traps and snares and dead ends gave them complete control over their environment.

He supposed that made sense. Someone was always trying to assassinate the elders, for old grievances or to steal their wealth or position. Being out in the open made them more vulnerable and gained them little, since masters could communicate with each other mentally without having to risk a trip away from home.

But he wasn't a master, and he wasn't old, and confined spaces to someone with a knight's training were just good opportunities to get ambushed.

Like right now, for instance.

"Nobody is sneaking up on us," Jerome assured him.

"How do you know?"

"I'd feel them."

The way you felt the last ones, Mircea didn't say, because it wouldn't help.

Like looking over your shoulder another few dozen times, he told himself sharply. You're a vampire, for God's sake. Use your senses!

But that was just it—mages could fool the senses, even vampire ones. Mircea had once believed that his new condition would make him invulnerable, from everyone except his own kind, at least. But he'd quickly discovered that that wasn't true at all. Humans outnumbered his people by a huge margin, so huge that breaking the secrecy laws and calling attention to yourself would get you a quick stake or a trip to see the sunrise. And those were just the normal kind of humans.

Magical ones were... something else. Something deadly, if they chose, and unlike his own power, which was relatively set, mages were constantly coming up with new spells, potions, and curses. Just because you were able to counter them one day didn't mean you'd have what it took the next. Not to mention that they bought and sold magic all the time, giving one man the power of many, should he have the wherewithal to purchase what he lacked.

Vampires had to earn their power, Mircea thought resentfully.

Mages just plucked down gold for it.

Gold they probably stole anyway.

From people foolish enough to frequent places like this.

"Let me do the talking," Jerome said, suddenly catching his arm.

Mircea looked up at the little bar they'd stopped outside of, and then back at his friend.

"I was planning to."

They went in.

The place was just as Mircea remembered it from a long-ago visit. Which was unfortunate, since it had been a pit. And the years had not been kind; it was still small, dark, and cramped, with funny, potion-like smells in the background, and tables so close together that it was hard to move between them. Although it would have been anyway, with the ceiling sagging so low in spots that a normal-sized man couldn't stand upright.

Mircea stifled a curse after bumping his head for the second time. Not because he was clumsy, but because the damned tavern was lit only by a small fireplace—too small. It left the corners in shadows so deep that even vampire eyes had trouble making them out.

Fortunately, nobody appeared to be hiding in them, because the place was all but empty. The few patrons sitting dispiritedly over their drinks never even looked up as they came in and made their way to one of the tables in the higher end of the room. The only person to notice was the barman, coming out of the back after a moment to slam down a couple of steins of the place's hideous... beer? Wine? Mircea had never been sure what it was meant to be. It smelled like a dead rat stewed in vinegar, so it was anyone's guess, but they had to pay an exorbitant price for it anyway.

It was the cost of admission, which was supposed to include a chance to speak to the proprietor.

Whoever that was tonight.

"Hieronimo?" Jerome asked, looking up with a friendly smile. "We'd like to—"

The barman left.

"—have a word," Jerome finished, with a twist to his lips.

"How can you trust someone when you don't even know his real name?" Mircea whispered, leaning over the table. Because they didn't. The man they'd met here before had informed them that 'Hieronimo' was simply a code word for whoever was on call that night.

The bar was a front for a group that sold advice, along with more unsavory things, to non-magic types with gold to waste, because God knew they couldn't make much off their beer. It had been a staple of the Venetian magical community for a few centuries now, but nobody knew much about the people who ran it, except that they all called themselves by their long-dead first proprietor's name for some reason that Mircea didn't know and didn't care about. But if you wanted answers from a mage—a good one—you paid for the beer, and you asked your questions, and were then quoted a price for additional services.

Assuming he bothered to talk to you at all, that is.

"I don't trust anyone but you," Jerome murmured. "That's why you're here. But I was told that the mages are on our side in this."

"Whatever this is," Mircea said, and got only a small smile in return.

Personally, he would have paid what little he had, and gladly, just for the chance to escape. But Dorina's fate hung in the balance, so he stayed, despite the chills crawling up and down his spine. The senate wanted Jerome's mission to succeed, and if Mircea helped, Jerome thought he could make a case for an exception to the kill-dhampirs-on-sight rule.

So this would work, Mircea would make it work, whatever the hell this was. Only he really wished he could get more than three words out of Jerome about it! But his friend had been abnormally close-lipped—like now, for instance.

"It will be fine," Jerome told him, because, yes, that helped.

Mircea shut up and drank beer to give himself something to do, grateful for once that he couldn't taste it.

Time passed.

More time passed.

The desire to get up and bolt grew—significantly.

Or maybe that was the beer. Mircea pushed the odorous substance away from him with a sound that made Jerome look up. And smile.

"It really is astonishing, isn't it?"

"At least tell me what happened to you," Mircea said, ignoring the attempt at inane conversation. "Or am I not allowed to know that, either?"

Jerome glanced around, but the two nefarious types at the other table had just left, leaving them momentarily alone in the small room. He lowered his voice anyway. "Somebody knew we were coming."

"How? You said yourself—"

"I don't know how. But it wasn't happenstance. No one tries to rob three masters—"

"Not if they're sane."

"—or carries that kind of firepower. They shouldn't even have had it!"

"You mean those things they were throwing at us?" Mircea made a quick gesture, slashing the air like lightning. He'd been in Venice too long; he was starting to talk with his hands like a local, but he didn't have a word for what he'd seen. "Those... bolts of power?"

Jerome nodded. "They took out both my men and would have killed me, too, if not for you."

Mircea blinked a little, not sure that Jerome realized what he'd just said. Those strange energy bolts had shattered some brick, cutting Mircea's face, and had left a hole in his cloak, which had annoyed him even more. Because his face had healed already, but that cloak was his best.

He'd been fretting over having to save up for a new one, since the burnt area wasn't near a seam or an edge and was thus impossible to repair discreetly. Or having to waste hours trawling through the pawn shops, trying to find a replacement without noticeable flaws. He hadn't thought that every bolt he dodged could have killed him.

He swallowed slightly, trying to remember how many of the damned things the masters had thrown.

Too many.

He suddenly wasn't feeling so well.

"You saved me," Jerome repeated, leaning over the table. "I won't forget that."

Mircea sipped his terrible-smelling drink some more, struggling not to show how shaken he was. "You, er, you were well hidden," he said, because Jerome was looking like he expected a response. "I... heard you calling in my head, but when I reached the pier, I couldn't find you. Until you appeared out of nowhere—"

Jerome shot him a smile. "It's my gift, remember?"

Mircea nodded, recalling the first time they'd met, as two supposedly weak, masterless vampires in one of the city's holding cells. Mircea had been exactly as he seemed, a down-on-his-luck baby vampire trying to survive in this new, cutthroat world, and not doing especially well at it. Jerome, on the other hand, had been in disguise, tracking a woman who had wronged his family more than a century before, because vampires have long memories.

Especially when someone kills their Sire.

Nonetheless, he shouldn't have been able to get away with it, since the power masters radiate was unmistakable, like ants on the skin. Fire ants, Mircea thought, resisting an impulse to rub his arms. It was a memory, however, not a current problem, because Jerome had an unusual skill.

He was the only vampire Mircea had ever met who had the ability to draw down his power, to mimic the level of any vampire he chose. He could feel like nobody and nothing, just a baby, completely unthreatening and harmless—to others of his kind, anyway. Who were so used to homing in on power signatures in battle, that they'd temporarily lost him when he went dim. And then disappeared into a crowd filled with actual young vampires on errands for their masters.

Mircea had found him shortly thereafter, zeroing in on

the mental cry for help that had echoed so loudly in his ears that he'd yelped and scared a shopkeeper. He'd quickly turned from hunting for deals among the pigment sellers of Venice to hunting Jerome. And had found him, just as one of the masters did.

They'd had to spread out to check every supposed baby vamp in the crowd, so he and Jerome had been left facing only one. Who still managed to gut Jerome before they killed him, but not before the vamp got off a cry for help of his own. Leaving Jerome and Mircea on a mad chase across the city, one they'd won only because they knew it better than those following them.

But it had been a very close thing.

Too close, not to know what was going on here.

Although considering where they were, Mircea already had a good idea.

"Those bolts they were throwing," he said softly. "They weren't master's powers, were they?"

He was talking about gifts, like Jerome's ability to fade, that upper-level masters sometimes developed over time. Gifts that seemed a lot like magic to Mircea. Not the kind the mages had—all flashy spells and fire magic, the kind that could incinerate a young vampire such as himself in a single blow, if they landed. But the kind that made sure they never would.

Mages could levitate things, using spells to send items soaring into the skies. But Mircea had seen a master lift a fully laden galley, unimaginably heavy and caught on a spur of rock, as if it was nothing. Allowing the damage to be fixed and the ship saved.

Mages could augment their speed with tricks, or tattoo their bodies with glyphs that gave them enhanced vision or scent. But masters could move faster than the average mage could see, like those the other night, who had crossed half a city before Mircea and Jerome could reach the next *sestiere*. They didn't need spells; they already had senses keener than a hound's nose or a hawk's eye.

Mages could change their appearance, altering it with potions and spells. But a master could reach into someone's mind and make them see whatever he wanted them to see. Mircea had found that he was especially good at that already, able to influence the minds of those around him in ways that others, even some far older than himself, could not. He suspected that, if he ever did manage to reach master status, that might be where his talent would lie.

But what he'd seen last night . . . that was not a master's power. Vampires were magical creatures, but even the best of them couldn't throw spells. That kind of magic was solely the purview of the mages.

So how had they managed it?

"That's what you're here for, isn't it?" he pressed, when Jerome just sat there.

Jerome looked uncomfortable, but he finally nodded. And then that voice came again, the one echoing in Mircea's head in a really uncomfortable way. Because Jerome wasn't going to discuss this aloud, even in whispers.

What you haven't heard, what almost no one knows who isn't there, is that we aren't winning against the rebels. We were, at first. Fought them to a standstill, killed off the leaders, thought that was it.

Mircea nodded. The rebellion that had broken out after the new consuls took power had been vicious but short, at least in vampire terms. It had taken six years, during which he'd fretted in Venice, unable to get back to his wife, because the fighting had raged fiercest in his old homeland. Travel had been forbidden, and by the time the ban was lifted—

He pushed the thought away abruptly. What was important now was Dorina. And this new information, which threatened the world they both lived in.

"It's started up again?" he asked.

Jerome's mouth tightened. *It never stopped. We may have killed a few leaders, but there were apparently many more we didn't know about. They went underground, made new plans—and new friends. And recently re-emerged...*

"And?" Mircea prompted, because Jerome's mental voice had petered out.

And it's a slaughter. We met them in combat two months ago, and we haven't won an encounter since. They've started exhibiting new skills—mage skills—like nothing we've ever seen. Not a potion bomb or some sort of spell object, such as could be bought and would run dry soon enough. But vampires wielding actual magic, just like a mage. Throwing spells and making wards as if they were born to it! And yet having all the powers of their vampire nature, as well.

"What?" Mircea just looked at him. He'd expected something to do with magic, but not that. Because that was impossible! "But . . . they're vampires. They *can't*—"

"I assure you, they can." Jerome's gray eyes were sober. *They're using it to push us back on almost all fronts. It's not general knowledge, because it just started happening, but it's only a matter of time before the news gets out. And if we don't stop it now, it won't be long before other masters hear of it—ones cowed by the senate at the moment, but unhappy with the new rules and restrictions on their behavior—and start joining the rebels.*

"They can't want to go back to that! To what we had!"

"Some do. Lawlessness is profitable." Jerome's mouth twisted. *And even those who don't... well. No one likes being on the losing side, now do they?*

He drank beer.

Mircea stared at him.

A man staggered out of the curtained room in back and fell over, a knife protruding from his back, his pale blue eyes confused and fogged and desperate.

It seemed Hieronimo had arrived.

CHAPTER EIGHT

Present Day, Dory
A couturier's shop on the Rue de Whatever, Paris

S top slapping at them, Dory!"

"Then tell them to stop touching me," I snarled. I already had a migraine, thanks to the happy little vision Dorina had gifted me with in the car on the way here. And now a bunch of animated pincushions were trying to stick me full of holes.

"They're just trying to measure you," Radu said, sounding impatient.

"I know my measurements!" I snapped, as another pincushion came flying at me, glittering with intent. And ended up nailed to the wall by a pair of scissors for its trouble.

It just stayed there, vibrating slightly, like a small, wounded animal.

A small, wounded animal with friends, I thought, as a half dozen others suddenly zoomed at me from all parts of the room.

"*Arrêtez!*"

The command cracked through the air, like a general commanding troops. Troops that suddenly stopped mid-flight, except for the two I was currently choking to death. They made puffy little wheezing noises through my fingers as a creature out of a sci-fi flick approached, gleaming in silver.

And plucked them out of my grip.

I didn't even protest, although the reflection of my features in his shiny, shiny coat looked a little pissed. Or maybe that was the distorting, fun-house effect of the thing, which was almost blinding under the harsh lights of the inner sanctum. He examined the pincushions while Radu tried to manhandle the scissors to release the other.

He failed, possibly because he was also babbling apologies a mile a minute at the same time.

I looked from him to the silver vision, complete with a butt-length fall of jet-black hair, silver banded shades, silver rings on silver-tipped hands, and a silver mess of a cravat, and decided it was a boy. Mainly because of the far too tight silver trousers, which ended in silver boots, of course. Thigh-high ones.

I was suddenly, vastly relieved that we weren't really here for clothes.

"It's of no consequence," the silver god glimmered at me, with a smile almost as predatory as a vamp's. "I have many senatorial clients. Although few, if I may say so, who are quite so charming."

He bent over my now empty hand, while Radu pursed his lips. And looked me up and down, as if trying to decide what Claude found charming about my ripped jeans and scuffed leather jacket full of weapons. I smirked at him over the great man's back and received a warning look for my trouble. Claude was Radu's personal couturier, and I had already been told what would happen if I upset him and got Radu banned.

"A medal?" I'd asked, and received a truly frightening look in return.

Radu did not play around when it came to clothes.

Although at least this cleared up the mystery of exactly where 'Du came up with some of his more memorable ensembles. In fact, I kind of thought I owed the guy an apology. I'd always thought him over the top, but if this was where he shopped, damned if he wasn't positively restrained.

We were in the back of a posh shop on the Avenue de Whatever, in Paris. I hadn't paid much attention because I'd been groggy from another wild ride in Dorina's messed-up memories. I didn't know why she kept plaguing me, especially now. Would it be too much to ask to maybe wait for the current crisis to pass before dredging up old ones?

Especially old, irrelevant ones.

Because whatever had happened way back when, it had obviously been dealt with. And while, under normal circumstances, I might have been interested in just how Mircea worked out a deal to keep a dhampir on the premises without getting staked, I was a little more worried about somebody else getting staked right now. Which is why I gritted my teeth and put up with the pincushions of doom, and the measuring tape they were towing around between them, that was getting up close and personal. Until they finally had the info they required for a wardrobe I couldn't afford and didn't need.

Yes, technically, I was a senator, brought on board by some of daddy's machinations to give his faction in the Senate the extra votes they needed during the war. But that was going to last all of about a nanosecond after said war ended, and what was I going to do with a bunch of couture then? I didn't need couture; I needed answers.

Which was why I escaped back out front as soon as possible, since nobody seemed to care about my personal opinions anyway.

Nobody followed me. And nobody was in the shop, probably because it was by invitation only. Claude—just Claude; like Madonna, he only needed one name—was a fixture in the world of paranormal couture, which was apparently as cutthroat as the human version. This place was a positive fortress of wards, in case the competition sneaked in to steal any of his designs, or the spells behind them. And, since the great man, or mage technically, slept over the shop in a luxury apartment protected by those same wards, bursting in to ask questions about his exclusive clientele wasn't as easy as one might think.

Even when one of those clients was a missing consul with questionable taste.

I didn't have anything else to do, so I drifted around,

examining the merchandise and studiously not looking out of the windows at the street across the way, where Marlowe and Elise—the French op—had staked out. They couldn't get in, at least not without an appointment, the nearest of which had been over a month away. But Radu, ex-king, brother of a senator, second-level master vamp, and rich as Croesus... well, he was another story.

Especially when he was dragging another senator, one in dire need of fashion help—his words to Claude—along with him.

So, we were in. I just didn't see what good that was doing when 'Du was talking taffeta vs. satin instead of anything useful about Louis-Cesare. I supposed he expected me to come up with some clues, but I honestly didn't see what. Other than slamming the big guy against a wall and threatening to rip his throat out if he didn't start talking, which apparently was right out when it came to well-connected mages.

Thus throwing out 90% of my skill set, I thought, checking out a flirty little dress, which appeared to be cussing at me.

It took me a minute to realize what was going on, and then I grinned. And the dress, which seemed to be a fabric version of a mood ring, grinned back. At least, the curse words, rain clouds, and rude gestures that had covered it a second ago were erased, to be replaced with the French words for amused, happy, and curious. Along with grinning suns, dancing flowers, and emojis.

And what the hell? As if Facebook and Twitter weren't bad enough, now I was supposed to want my innermost emotions flaunted to everybody who saw me? Seriously?

A bunch of question marks spiraled up out of the white background, along with the French words for confused, unsure, and bewildered. Until I thrust it back on the rack and stepped away, because I had enough trouble with diplomacy as it was. I didn't need everybody knowing I was about to belt them even before I did!

The rest of the offerings were equally head-scratching, at least to me, because this wasn't my world. Wasn't even close to my world, I thought, checking out some eye-searingly yellow, very high-heeled, wedge-type shoes with built-in bird cages in the soles, complete with little hopping, tweeting birdies that I really hoped weren't real. Or if you didn't like those, there were blue ones with tiny aquariums in the soles, complete with—you guessed it—very confused-looking fish. Or some pink-and-white ones with animated wooden carousel horses affixed to the bottoms, which apparently trotted you around the cobblestones.

I stared at them, wondering what happened if you fell down. Did they just keep going? Galloping through the streets while you screamed your head off, bump, bump, bumping along behind?

Because, if so, there were a couple of Christmas presents sorted out early.

The shoes matched dresses with similar embroidered motifs: yellow birds flitting across white brocade; green, red, and white fish swimming around aquamarine silk; and sleek horses with embroidered manes flowing, their jeweled eyes flashing, their silver harnesses gleaming as they rotated around a golden carousel of a skirt. They were impressive, in a strictly artsy kind of way. Like, I could admire the creativity that went into them, and the spells that animated them, the same way I'd admire a painting on the wall of an art gallery. But I wouldn't want to wear it.

Seriously, they were tacky as hell.

The only things I saw that weren't were some surprisingly toned-down items in the same silver stuff Claude had been sporting. Including a jumpsuit that wasn't half bad. It was too shiny, almost mirror-like, but the cut was interesting—if I had a reason to need a bright silver, one-shouldered, mid-drift-baring, tight-assed jumpsuit.

Bet I could work it, though, I thought, before I caught myself.

I started to put it back when some movement caught my eye. I swung around to see a line of other outfits, different in style but with that same shiny, metallic cloth, in the window. All of which were currently wearing my face.

I blinked at the nearest one, and it blinked back, my startled eyes winking at me off a mannequin's pert backside. Ooookay, I thought, staring around. And noticing that the silver stuff was a lot more prominent than I'd thought, hanging off racks and draping languid-looking models, meaning that a hundred startled Dorys were all suddenly staring at me.

Once again, I started to put the jumpsuit back where I'd found it, only to have what looked like the whole room skew wildly as it followed the motion. And then change to images of my belly button, a hundred tiny navels peering over the top of my low-cut jeans. I jumped back, letting go of the weirdo fabric in the process, and everything abruptly blanked again.

Leaving just a sea of shiny, shiny silver and me, with no weird-ass reflections.

Not even in the ones in the window, where the images had been clearer than the rest, maybe because I was standing closer...

My thoughts broke off at the sight of Marlowe, across the street outside, making faces at me. I didn't know what was wrong with him for a minute, because he looked deranged. Gesturing and thumping his head and dancing around—

And then I got it. He was trying to talk to me mentally, but it wasn't working. Dorina could do that shit, but I couldn't. A fact which, for once, I was pretty happy about, because he looked livid. Like he thought I was playing around, clothes shopping, instead of doing the job, and screw him. I wanted Louis-Cesare back more than he did, but the clothes *were* the job. Because what the hell else was there to look at in a damned couturier's?

If this place even meant anything, and I didn't know that it did. Anthony could have come for his regular appointment, then gone somewhere else and been attacked, or whatever the hell had happened to him. Likewise, Louis-Cesare could have come here because it was the last place Anthony was seen, just like we had.

But, in that case, why did he also disappear?

It could be mere coincidence. Louis-Cesare had been

Anthony's senator for years, and the two of them had once been pretty close. It seemed at least possible that he'd had an idea after he left here, checked it out, and gotten lucky.

Or unlucky, considering that he was now missing, too.

Of course, he might have also picked up on something while here that gave him a clue, but if so, I wasn't seeing it.

I wasn't seeing much of anything except for a bunch of really tacky clothes.

And Marlowe, making a fool of himself in the street.

I grabbed the jumpsuit again with one hand, and with the other, I sent a whole line of one-fingered salutes at Marlowe, from the surface of every outfit in the window.

And, okay, yeah. Now he was pissed. And coming over here, only he forgot about—

"Dory. What are you doing?" That was Radu.

"Nothing," I said, folding the finger under about the time Marlowe hit the wards outside. And got his little curly do even curlier as a result.

I grinned, he smoked, and 'Du took the jumpsuit away from me, holding it up to the light.

And now we were surrounded by frowny-faced Radus, all peering into the fabric as if looking for a zit.

As if such a thing would dare to sully the pristine perfection, I thought.

"What is this?"

"Ah," Claude said, wafting in, despite wearing heels that would have defied even a supermodel. "Like father, like son."

"What?" All the little Radus suddenly perked up.

"Your son, Louis-Cesare?"

Radu and I nodded.

"He absolutely fell in love with this design. To the point that he ran off with one of my prototypes, the naughty boy." He leaned in to Radu. "Don't worry. I added it to your account."

Radu waved it away. "A prototype? Then these," an elegant gesture took in the wide range of silver designs, "aren't finished?"

"Oh, these," Claude sighed and rolled his eyes. "What one does to sustain the process of creation. No. I meant one of the special ones, the kind of thing I do for elite clients."

"Elite clients?" I asked, stupidly getting my hopes up.

"Such as yourself, dear Dorina." He smiled that predatory smile at me. "And Anthony, of course."

CHAPTER NINE

1457, Mircea
A terrible bar in Venice, Italy

All right, what now?" Jerome asked, as the curtain swished closed behind them.

It had done that on its own, as soon as they stumbled into the back room of the little bar. That normally would have been cause for some concern, except that Mircea's concern was already busy, focused on the group of heavily armed mages who had just run through the front door and almost succeeded in killing them, only they'd underestimated vampire speed.

Just as he had underestimated mage... oddness... because there was no back door.

"You're asking *me*?" Mircea said, looking around for an exit that remained stubbornly absent, his arms full of a dying mage, as an energy bolt fluttered the curtain on the other side.

Fluttered but didn't destroy, because Hieronimo must have spelled the place, although that made no damned sense. If it was spelled so that no one could get in, then how had he gotten stabbed? Because Mircea, Jerome, and Hieromino's soon-to-be corpse were in the same room, the man must have just been knifed in, yet no one was there. And since there was no back door, it rather seemed like the man must have stabbed himself.

Although this was a mage establishment, so who the hell knew?

Jerome must have had the same thought, because he was staring around as well, as if expecting to be jumped at any moment. While spell after spell hammered at the ephemeral-looking curtain, which shuddered but somehow held, a fact that threatened to break Mircea's brain. He could see the damned mages on the other side, through the thin weave, a bar full of them now.

Which meant this bolt-hole of theirs was about to turn into a grave.

"This is your mission!" he hissed at Jerome. "*Do* something!"

Jerome went from staring at the curtain to staring at him, and for the first time since he arrived, the self-assured master vampire was gone. Replaced by the wide-eyed innocent Mircea had met in a Venetian prison cell. Mircea had once thought, after his friend's true age and status had been revealed, that the act had been impressive, practically flawless over weeks of close contact.

Now he wondered how much Jerome had been acting, and how much of that was simply who he was at heart, something that might have been endearing if it wasn't about to get them both killed.

"You're the soldier," Jerome said, licking his lips. "I'm the spy. I'm just supposed to gather information. I don't deal with things like this!"

Wonderful.

"Here." Mircea thrust the mage into Jerome's arms and started crawling around the floor.

Jerome watched him, his face tense and pale, his hands covered in the man's blood. "W-what do I do with him?"

"Bring him around! I have a question," Mircea said grimly, knocking on wood.

The *crash, crash, crash* of spells against the flimsy barrier seemed to be getting louder, which likely wasn't a good sign. But Mircea couldn't reinforce it because he wasn't a mage, damn it! But he was a vampire, so he used what skills he did have.

Not that any of them helped much, either.

The floor was solid, with no big, echoing spaces

underneath. The same was true for the old stone walls, which didn't even have the expected insects or rats scurrying about —surprising, considering the state of this place. But then again, maybe not. Because, at the lowest range of his hearing, something that would have been entirely silent to a human, there it was: the telltale buzz of a ward.

Mircea cursed inventively.

It wasn't just over the door; it was over everything. Meaning that he couldn't just punch a new exit through the thick old stones, even assuming he had time for that. He had seconds to figure a way out of this, to find something that would trigger a way out, assuming the damned place had one! But the myriad items on a long counter and some rickety shelves weren't helping.

There were jars and bottles of odd-smelling powders, vials of multicolored brews, most of which stunk to high heaven, and baskets of dried flowers and herbs. There were iron... thingies... in a basket and some wooden... sticks... in a box, and a bunch of amulets hung on a board, and damn it all! There had to be something here! Something the still unconscious mage couldn't tell them...

Or maybe he already had.

Mircea stopped suddenly, realizing that they had already passed through the ward when they ran in here. Just as Hieronimo had when he stumbled through the curtain. And if the mage had done anything to facilitate that, it hadn't been apparent.

He'd been busy dying at the time.

So it was on him.

"What are you doing?" Jerome asked, as Mircea pushed him out of the way and knelt by the mage.

Jerome had laid him face down on the floor and ripped open his shirt, but had yet to remove the knife. Probably afraid the man would bleed out if he did. Mircea, who had a small healing gift, would have tried to help him, but there was no time. The ward was going to fail any moment, and if they were still here when it did, there wouldn't be help for any of them.

"Mircea—" Jerome said, staring at the curtain.

"I know." Mircea's hands deftly searched the mage, looking for a way out, a weapon, anything at all.

And to his surprise, he found one.

Or he found something, anyway.

The mage had a thick gold chain around his neck, heavy, exquisite work, the kind of thing a noble might wear. Yet it was hung with a plain rock crystal pendant. It looked like those hawkers sold to the festival crowds, carved with the face of a saint, along with cheap glass rosaries, pilgrim badges, and tiny silver crosses. It was not something that belonged on that chain.

Until Mircea pressed it, while searching for a catch or an opening.

And found more than he bargained for.

The stone started glowing with an intense yellow light that spilled over the dirty floor and highlighted Jerome's anxious face. And probably his own, because Mircea had no idea what it was. Or why it was now emitting some kind of odd noise.

"Is it important?" Jerome asked breathlessly. He'd always had trouble remembering that vampires don't need to breathe.

"I don't know." Mircea turned it over, looking for he knew not what. Instructions? An incantation? Any damned thing to get them out of here—

"I think it's important!" Jerome yelled, his hair blowing everywhere and his face suddenly whiting out.

Because a swirling circle of light had just appeared out of nothing in the middle of the room, with a terrifying *drum, drum, drum* sound that was so loud, it even drowned out the sound of the spells being lobbed outside. Which, judging by the colors suddenly exploding against the curtain, had just increased exponentially.

"I think it's a portal!" Jerome yelled, staring at it with huge eyes.

"What?"

"A gateway! I've heard of them before!"

"A gateway to where?"

"I don't know!"

He stared at Mircea, and Mircea stared back. Because jumping into what looked like an inferno, going who-knew-where was not either man's idea of fun. Of course, neither was staying here.

And then the decision was made for them when the curtain abruptly gave way. Jerome screamed, Mircea cursed, and a barrage of spells hit shelves, exploding them into stinging, noxious, multicolored clouds. And a second later, he and Jerome and an almost-corpse were falling through wind and light and sound, screaming their heads off.

Except for the corpse, of course.

"Aaaaahhhhh!"

Thud.

"Aaahhhh!"

Crash.

"Aaaaaahhhhh!"

Squelch.

"Ahh." That last was Jerome, who had landed on top of Mircea, who had landed on top of Hieronimo, who had landed in a pile of fish guts. A deep pile, which was why Mircea was no longer screaming—his head had gone under.

He came up, gasping, not for breath but because that's what you do when there are fish intestines on your face and what turned out to be an eyeball in your mouth.

"Gah!" He spat it out and sat up, staring around. And through hanging strands of innards saw what looked like a port.

"Where are we?" he asked Jerome, who was flailing about, trying to get out of the slippery substance.

"It… it looks like a port."

Thank you, Mircea thought evilly, and got up.

He rescued the corpse, in case it wasn't one yet, turning it right side up. But he didn't do anything else, because he didn't have time. Not because any of the mages had followed them through the portal, which had just winked out. But because there were plenty of others on this side, yelling and scuffling and fighting, in and among a group of dark buildings and out onto moonlit sand.

One of whom had just grabbed Jerome.

"Aahh!" Jerome said, which did not help.

Of course, neither did Mircea's attempt to drain the mage, at least enough for them to get away.

It did seem to make him angry, though.

"Shields, scum," the mage snarled, and the next thing Mircea knew, he was thrown against a wall and pinned there by an unseen hand.

It appeared to be trying to choke him to death, which wouldn't work, or possibly to pop his head off, which might. Mircea started thrashing around, trying to get some kind of leverage, and failing rather spectacularly since his feet couldn't even touch the ground. But Jerome's could, and fortunately, he took that moment to remember that he was a master.

The mage went flying, Mircea hit wet dirt, and Jerome screamed some more, because this really wasn't his forte. But it didn't interfere with his abilities any, which was why the mage splashed down a safe distance away, in the midst of dark ships, darker water, and bright spells. The latter were flashing here and there and everywhere, lighting up the night. It would have been oddly beautiful if they weren't so deadly.

"Get down!" Mircea told Jerome, who was just standing there.

Jerome got down. And grabbed Hieronimo, before following Mircea's crawl along a mud, blood, and fish-filled bank. Some fishermen had cleaned their catch hours earlier and left the waste for the tide to take. But it wasn't time for the tide, which didn't seem to have gotten all of the last batch, in any case. And it was fairly odorous after baking in the Venetian sun. Add in the smell of the sea and the odd, lightning-scent of the magic being flung around, and Mircea was almost scent-blind.

It made him want to get out of here even more.

The question was, which direction wouldn't get them

killed?

Because the fight seemed to be everywhere.

It must have been how Hieronimo was injured; he'd been caught up in the battle, which was why he'd been late for his meeting with Jerome. And had used the portal stone to escape, only not before he was seriously injured. But they couldn't use the same means to return, since there were enemies at the bar now, too.

But they also couldn't stay here.

"Is the mage dead?" Mircea whispered to Jerome once they found a temporary bolt-hole behind some barrels.

"What?"

"The mage! Did you kill him?"

"Oh." Jerome swallowed and then shook his head. "No, I don't think so. I just threw him as hard as I could. He landed in the water, but I'm not sure where."

Mircea couldn't blame him for that. Mages were hitting the water all the time, falling off of ships and being blown back into rigging, where fires were starting to break out. The blazes were small at the moment, but they wouldn't stay that way.

And even if they did, somebody was going to sound an alarm before long. Mircea had finally recognized this place, a prominent beach on the lagoon where ships of all types regularly anchored. That included humble fishing boats, rotund merchant ships, tiny skiffs used for shooting water birds, and gondolas. But there were also several sleek warships, their dark hulls blocking out the moonlight and towering above the scene.

They would almost certainly have a skeleton crew aboard, even if none of the others did.

Time to go.

Or it would have been, had Hieronimo not taken that moment to come around. "Mircea..." The man's hand caught his sleeve.

"Stay still."

Mircea gripped the man's shoulder and concentrated, trying to will some life into the abused body. He didn't know that it would be enough; his ability was limited, and he'd never tried to help anyone hurt this badly before. But it seemed to be doing something, because the mage began breathing easier after a moment.

"Should . . . should we take the knife out?" Jerome asked, looking from the mage to Mircea.

But Hieronimo shook his head, grinning strangely out of lips already turning blue. "A little late for that. Looks like . . . you're on your own."

"On my own for what?" Jerome said. "I was told to meet with you, that you would help me find—"

"Do I look able to help anyone, boy?"

"I'm not a boy."

"Then stop acting like one!" The mage stopped for a coughing fit he couldn't afford, because Mircea was pretty sure the man was right. He was fading; most of the bleeding they'd tried to avoid making worse had just gone inside. Mircea could feel it, pooling low in the man's abdomen. He had minutes left, at most.

"What do you want to tell us?" he asked softly.

"See the ship with the lion flag? Fat merchant, riding low."

Mircea glanced over his shoulder and nodded. The merchant vessel flew the lion of St. Mark's, its crimson and gold motif lit by spellfire.

"Bunch of witches in the hold. Have to get them out. Have to rescue—" Another coughing fit erupted.

"How are we supposed to do that?" Jerome asked. "And even if we could, I didn't come here for witches! I came—"

"To stop a war."

Jerome nodded.

"Then you need those witches. They're the key, boy. Lover's Knot..." He trailed off, and Mircea was afraid it might be for the last time.

"Hieronimo!" He tried willing some more energy into him, but he was pretty sure it was too late. Too much damage for the body to heal meant he was just draining himself to no purpose.

But Jerome wasn't giving up so easily. "Hieronimo! We don't understand magic, either of us! We don't know what that means. You have to—"

"Stop telling me what I have to do," the man said, bloodshot blue eyes opening to glare at the small blond. "The only thing I have to do is die. You have to get those witches. The spell you want isn't in a grimoire or anybody's head. It was once, but it was destroyed. Now the only place to find it is *on them*. Help my people get them out; they can do the rest. But be careful; remember, what happens to one, happens to both..."

"What does?" Mircea shook him when he trailed off again, because it couldn't hurt at this point. "Hieromino! What does?"

But there was no reply, nor would there be.

The man was dead.

And this time, it was Jerome's turn to swear.

CHAPTER TEN

Present Day, Dory
Still at an overpriced dress shop, Paris

I t's fine," someone was saying. "She does this from time to time. No need for concern."

"Are you sure?" Someone else sounded doubtful. I opened my eyes to see my confused, slightly distorted-looking face staring back at me, out of a sea of shiny silver. "Perhaps some brandy?"

"That would be perfect."

My face drew back abruptly, into the silver field stretching across Claude's impressive pecs, and then disappeared entirely as the great man hurried off. Leaving me looking at Radu's worried features instead, bending over to peer at me. "*Are* you all right?"

"Yeah." I swallowed and sat up a little straighter in the chair somebody had found for me, and wished for something stronger than brandy.

I felt like death.

"Then what is all this?" Radu demanded in a whisper.

"Dorina. She keeps knocking me out to show me stuff."

"What kind of stuff?"

"I don't know! Weird stuff," I snapped, because my head was killing me. And because how the hell should I know?

And then there was brandy, which was tasty, if nothing else. Claude didn't serve the cheap stuff. I drank it while Radu questioned the great man about his clothes, something I was barely listening to because my brain was trying to beat its way out of my skull.

Until I finished my drink, and realized that Claude was *still talking.*

"—think a spell is a single object, a whole cloth, if you will. When, of course, that isn't true at all." He looked at me archly, pleased to have a new pupil. "Roman matrons, you know."

"What?"

He jerked over a rack with a bunch of bright yellow garments swinging from it. "Chinese silk," he said dramatically. "Highly prized in old Rome."

"Okay."

"But hugely expensive. Had to come along the Silk Road." A dark eyebrow arched expressively. "Bandits, you know."

"Uh huh."

"As a result, the end price was enough to make even royalty blanch. So what did they do, hm?"

I looked at him blearily. "No idea."

"They pulled a thread." Claude picked out a cheongsam-style dress with gamboling dragons—literally, they were chasing each other about, playing some sort of game involving a red ball and a lot of fire-breathing. I jerked back to avoid one miniature flame, and wondered how the hell you were supposed to wear that and not burn the house down!

Claude was frowning at it, too, but for different reasons. He took out a tiny pair of silver scissors and *snicked* away a single, trailing strand, holding it up to the light. "Or, to be more precise, they had their slaves do it," he informed me. "Carefully picking apart the so-precious cloth, which the Romans had no way to make for themselves at the time. But they knew how to get what they wanted, nonetheless—"

"By destroying it?"

A diamond-encrusted finger pressed against my lips. "No. By remaking it. Into filmy, gossamer garments, three and four and even more, all from a single piece of good, thick silk. They took what they wanted from the original creation and made it their own."

I moved the finger, so I could push my lips past. "Okay, but what does that—"

"Unh, unh, unh. You haven't let me finish."

The finger was back.

Any second now, I was going to bite it off.

"I read that story some years ago, as a young designer, and it stuck with me. It's the reason for much of my success. Well, that and talent, of course. But even talent needs help—"

"Which you found in old types of cloth?" Radu asked, looking me a warning.

Probably because my fangs were out.

I drew them back in.

"Which I found in old types of *spells*. After all, they're made of threads, too, *n'est ce pas*? Myriad ones, each serving a different function, contributing to the whole. We don't think of them that way anymore, and why should we? We learn them as children, toddling about. Say this, and your magic does that. Simple, *non*?"

"*Non*. We're not mages," I reminded him, after capturing the hand so it wouldn't tempt me again.

But Claude apparently mistook the gesture and brought my clenched fist up to kiss it. "Of course you aren't, dear girl. But I can assure you, most mages never think about their spells, much less what goes into them. Just as most people never think that you aren't wearing a shirt, you are wearing a few thousand threads, arranged in a pattern."

"But you thought of it."

"Yes, and it changed my life! All of a sudden, I was seeing it everywhere—"

"Seeing... what?" I asked, confused. Because Claude's method of delivery was a lot like Radu's.

"Inspiration!" Claude abruptly released me and strode away. "Come, come!"

We came, came.

"I find it in all sorts of places," he told us, throwing the words over his shoulder as we headed back into the workroom.

"The wards on venerable buildings, maintained but never upgraded; the incantations scribbled on a bit of parchment encased in ancient amulets; the dusty old grimoires in the back of tiny, used bookshops that no one ever bothers to dig out of crumbling piles. All of them, in their own way, they speak to me!"

"And tell you to make them into... those?" I asked, glancing back at the mirrored outfits. Because it all sounded very cool, but the end result was a little anticlimactic. Like watching a bunch of TVs in a shop window, all set to the same channel.

"Oh, those," he waved them away. "I use them at the beginning of my shows, to project the *motif du saison* on dozens of models, all at once: roaring lions; crashing waves; a perfect orchid branch, shivering in the breeze..."

"A single plum, floating in perfume, served in a man's— ow!" I said because Radu had just stepped on my foot.

"It makes for quite a start," Claude said, oblivious. "A line of pretty girls or handsome boys, coming down the runway with beautiful clothing, all shifting and changing in time to the music. I've received standing ovations."

"They're, uh, they're very nice," I said, because I wanted to be able to walk tomorrow.

He whirled on me. "But they are nothing! Merely a single strand of a far more intricate pattern. One note out of a symphony. Unlike this!"

And with that, a curtain was thrown back, with the flourish one might have used to reveal a recently discovered Da Vinci.

Claude struck a pose.

Radu and I peered into the little closet that had been revealed.

And then at each other.

And then back into the closet again.

"Armand!" Claude called when it became painfully obvious that we didn't get it.

Maybe because "it" was a bunch of fairly normal formal

wear, with nothing to recommend it that I could see, except maybe the cut. The cut was nice. Or maybe I was just too much of a philistine to understand.

Only if I was, it ran in the family.

Because Radu was looking bewildered as well.

A tall, skinny young man with a buzz cut ran in, scratching a zit. "*M'sieur*?"

"Stop that!" Claude hissed, slapping his hand. "Our guests would like a demonstration of the consular line."

Armand stopped scratching the zit. And grabbed a tuxedo jacket off a hanger, pulling it on over his Metallica T-shirt and jeans, which wasn't a bad look. But apparently wasn't the point either.

"*Allez!*" Claude made a gesture, and the boy allezed. Out of the shop and down the street, where he almost crashed into Marlowe, who was still lurking about, pretending to be James Bond.

And still smoking a little.

I grinned.

The boy dodged and jogged on, before stopping to pet a mangy-looking cat and almost getting run over by a guy on a bike.

I knew all this because I was seeing it. Not through the windows, which I couldn't see from here, and not in some kind of Dorina-induced vision. But in the lining of a woman's cape that Claude was helpfully holding up.

On the outside, it was fairly normal-looking: black velvet and floor-length, the kind you might wear over a ball gown if you were feeling particularly witchy. But on the inside, it was full-on cinema, not a mere reflection of what was in front of it, but an almost 360-degree view of everything around the boy.

Including the huge fist now headed toward his face, because the kid had gotten into a fight with the guy on the bike.

Claude made a sound of disgust and quickly closed the cape, smiling that huge, fake smile at me. "You see?"

"Not really," I said. Because a few GoPros could do the

same thing. Or one of those helmets the Google Earth guys wore, which, admittedly, were seriously dorky. But after seeing some of Claude's stuff—

Radu pushed me behind him.

"Anthony asked for these?"

Claude nodded. "He saw the ones outside and fell in love. I told him they only utilized a fraction of the original spell, and he simply had to know what else was possible."

"And you showed him."

The great man's face took on a long-suffering expression. "It was so much work, I can't begin to tell you. And I was in the middle of the winter line! But it was Anthony, so I pushed myself. And a few weeks later I had a prototype—and he was *overcome*. Wanted to outfit the entire court! Well, those with partners, at least. You know that they're always looking for new amusements?"

Radu nodded.

"Well, he's planning a scavenger hunt! But instead of things, people will hunt for les *amoureux*. He's building some sort of maze, there at court, and everyone will wear a piece of my special line, allowing them to see what their sweetheart sees. The first twenty or so to find each other will win a prize!"

I managed not to roll my eyes, but it was close.

Because no.

Radu just frowned slightly. "Then this spell, it only works on lovers?"

Claude nodded. "Yes, I warned Anthony about that. What if someone is involved with more than one person? I asked. It could become... awkward... if a pairing turned out to be a threesome! Or if a man goes looking for his wife and ends up finding his mistress! Or if the spell doesn't work because *l'amour*, it has faded. I told him he was playing with fire, but you know Anthony."

"Mm," Radu said, as the great man went to fetch the jacket from his returning assistant, and to berate him for getting it ripped in the scuffle.

"Anthony isn't doing a scavenger hunt," I told Radu in an undertone.

"What? Oh, of course not."

"Which raises the question, just how 'in love' do people have to be for this to work? One true pairing stuff, or..."

A magnificent eyebrow raised. "A night of passion with one of Anthony's famous beauties?"

"Followed by a 'forgotten' bit of clothing left behind?"

"It wouldn't need to be. Once the connection was established, some of their own clothes—or jewels or anything else they owned—could be spelled as a sort of one-way mirror into their lives."

I blinked because I kept forgetting that Radu did this sort of R&D for the senate all the time. Finding unusual answers to problems was his job when he wasn't being Mircea's flashy younger brother. I suddenly wondered if that was one reason he was a clothes horse: to give him access to creative geniuses who didn't know what they had.

"And wards won't pick it up, as it isn't a known surveillance spell," he added.

"So Anthony could infiltrate any of the rival courts, during the war talks, see what they're really planning?"

"Or hear." Radu's head tilted thoughtfully. "Claude?"

"My dear?"

"You wouldn't be able to make one of these with just sound, would you? I'm thinking about introducing Anthony's game to our court, but sight seems too easy."

And apparently, those were the magic words, because the great man lit up like the sun. "*My dear*. I'm sure I could. Anthony mentioned something of the kind himself, but I haven't had time. It's such an elaborate spell—so many threads! I've only begun to pull at them..."

Claude glided to a desk in a corner and started sorting through the piles. Unlike the workroom, which was almost fanatically clean and organized, the desk was a mess of sketches, fabric swatches, notes, and books. Including a huge, fat old thing stuffed with a bunch of mismatched pages that looked like they'd been torn from other volumes.

Some were typewritten, all nice and neat and modern, but most were older, the pages yellowed or moth-eaten or both. And a few, like the one he stopped on after a brief search, weren't paper at all, but vellum, a half-burnt piece of scraped-down animal hide that looked like it had been sourced from the pages of an illuminated manuscript. One made by a monk with issues.

There were no bright jewel tones or whimsical animals or pictures of hardy peasants here. Instead, it was all deep blue, gold, and black, with the gold mostly used to pick out the slanted eyes or accentuate the hooves on the demonic little creatures who scampered around, doing creepy stuff. Like stretching people on racks, their pale bodies showing up starkly against the dark background, or boiling them in oil, or pulling their guts out, all while grinning delightedly at the viewer.

As if to say, don't you wish you were here?

No. No, I don't, I thought, as Claude prattled on. There was something disturbing about them, more than just the obvious contrast of the badly drawn, almost cartoonish figures, and what they were doing. Something that made my hair stand up and my skin tighten. Like the piece of parchment they were written on. Which, when it caught the light just right, bore what looked like a scar and part of a tattoo, hidden under all that ink.

I shivered.

"Only the one page survived, I'm afraid," Claude said cheerfully. "Leaving me with but part of a spell to work with. Or part of a curse, as it was originally. I think it was based on demon magic—"

"What gave it away?" I asked hoarsely.

Radu kicked me.

But Claude mistook the question for interest. He beamed at me. "The method of transmission. Curses are like viruses, you know: they need a pathway into your magic. It's what feeds them, after the initial energy of the spell is expended; they literally torture you with your own power!" He looked appreciative of the ingenuity.

Radu started to look disturbed.

Like maybe he hadn't known that his couturier dabbled in demonology.

"In any case, whoever invented the original curse knew something about demons," Claude told us. "Specifically, incubi. And employed their method of penetrating the body's defenses and gaining access to a person's magic."

"And that method was..." I prompted.

"Why, emotion, of course! *L'amour*. That's why it only works on those with a close, personal bond."

"And why it's called Lover's Knot," Radu said, frowning at the page.

"What?" I realized that maybe I should have been paying attention to the text, instead of the freaky decorations.

"*Nodo d'amore*," Claude agreed, looking at me. "It's an Italian spell. Have you heard of it?"

I didn't answer. I was suddenly seeing a moonlit port, a dying man, and a haze of spellfire. And wondering if Dorina had been trying to tell me something useful, after all. But our communication sucked, and I wasn't sure what yet.

And it wasn't like I had any way to ask.

"I heard it was dangerous," I said, because both men were looking at me.

"Oh, not any more." Claude patted my hand reassuringly. "I was able to recreate it, even with so little to go on—all you have to do is follow the pattern, you know. But I didn't use anything like the whole spell. It's so intricate, it will take years to explore. But if it results in my designs being showcased in two courts..." His breath trembled slightly at the thought.

Radu smiled at him. "And who deserves it more? You say this design entranced my son?"

"Yes, indeed." Claude nodded proudly. "He ran off with the twin to Anthony's costume, something about wanting to see if it worked. I told him my designs always work, but there you are. I suppose he had to see for himself!"

"Ran off with... what, again?"

"Anthony was in the middle of a fitting when he received some kind of communication." Claude tapped his head solemnly. "The way vampires do."

Radu nodded.

"Well, he left immediately, still wearing his suit. Louis-Cesare took the other half of the pairing, the dress belonging to *la reine*, to see if he could trace him."

"Because it showed him what Anthony saw," I said, exchanging looks with Radu.

Okay, getting excited now.

And I guess Radu was, too, because the smile he turned on Claude was blinding. "What fun! I would so enjoy trying that myself. You wouldn't happen to have another item we could borrow, would you?"

"Another item?"

"From Anthony's set?"

Claude looked from Radu to me and back again. "But that was what? A week ago? You'll follow it to the laundry, *non*?"

"Perhaps. But I would still like to try."

Claude looked confused, but he appeared to be familiar with the eccentricities of his patrons, because it didn't last long. But instead of another one of those fake smiles, Radu received an apologetic frown. "You know there is nothing I would like better than to oblige you, my dear Radu. But there is nothing left. And I would need at least half of a pairing here in order to create another. Now, if Anthony—"

"I believe he is busy at the moment," Radu interrupted smoothly. "However, Dory and Louis-Cesare are lovers."

Claude looked at me in surprise. "*Vraiment?*" And then he smiled. And, for the first time, it actually looked genuine. I guess it's true what they say about the French and *l'amour*.

Or maybe he was seeing a six-figure wedding gown in my future.

"How *divine*," he gushed. "In that case, choose a garment, my dear. Just anything you like."

My motto has always been that I'll stop wearing black when they make a darker shade, but considering we were after a clear image here, I went with a bright silver top instead. And watched impatiently as Claude did his thing, with a wand, no less. But all the muttering and waving about didn't seem to help. Because the shirt shimmered and shook and flickered—and stayed the same.

Claude looked chagrined, and a slight flush appeared on the powdered cheeks. "My dear. I am *so* sorry."

I frowned. "It didn't work?"

"These things happen, you know. I wouldn't let it make me feel—"

"Why didn't it work?"

He stopped and looked at me awkwardly. "Sometimes, the affections, they can be a bit... one-sided—"

"One-sided?" I scowled. "You did it wrong. Do it again!"

The awkward slipped into the tragic. "I am afraid the outcome would be the same. The spell, you see, it has to have something to work with—"

"It has plenty to work with!"

"—on both sides—"

I growled at him because I was perilously close to going with option one. And slamming the great man against a wall and demanding that he find a way to make this happen. Which wouldn't help, but neither was this!

Radu stepped in. "Perhaps you could try it on me? Louis-Cesare is my Child. Our bond is strong."

"It's usually done with lovers," Claude said doubtfully. "But I could try."

More waving and incantation muttering followed. I didn't say anything, but if it worked for Radu and it didn't for me... I bit my lip and didn't say anything.

But the top stayed stubbornly silver.

Radu frowned at it. "You said the original was a curse?"

Claude nodded. "Oh, yes, a nasty one! It bound two people to the same fate. I think it was used as a torture spell once, a way of getting someone to break by letting them know that whatever unpleasantness was being inflicted on them was acting on their beloved, as well."

"What happens to one happens to both," I said, suddenly remembering something a long-dead mage had said.

"Yes, barbaric times." Claude shuddered delicately. "But, of course, I stripped all that out—"

"Can you put it back?"

"What?"

I grabbed his arm. "Can you put the original spell on me?"

"You want me to *curse* you?" The pretty blue eyes behind all the liner were suddenly wide and startled, probably because my fangs were out again. "Whatever for?"

I looked at 'Du. "I have an idea."

CHAPTER ELEVEN

1457, Mircea
A burning ship in the Lagoon, Venice, Italy

H-have I mentioned how much I hate fire?" Jerome said, jerking his cape closer around him.

"A few dozen times," Mircea said, through gritted teeth. Because he didn't love it any better.

"Oh, good. Just wanted to make that clear," Jerome said, and then gave a little scream when some burning rigging fell on him.

Mircea pulled it off and sent it flying at a sailor coming at them with a cudgel. And watched him go up in flames, because he was a vampire, too. And then watched him put out said flames with a muttered word, because he wasn't a normal vampire.

Mircea cursed and hit the deck behind some barrels, which exploded a second later as a spell hit them—the kind his people weren't supposed to be able to throw. And which caused him to scurry away, toward the bow of the ship, in the exact opposite direction from Jerome. And from where they needed to go.

The good news was that the shipload of magical vamps all seemed to be following him, giving Jerome a clear shot at the hold.

The bad news was that the shipload of magical vamps all seemed to be following him.

And were intent on using him to test out their shiny new powers. Because killing him the old-fashioned way wouldn't be nearly as much fun, would it, Mircea thought grimly, as a dozen burning barrels came hurtling his way. And shattered against the deck and mast and his legs as he dove under a furled sail.

And watched blowing bits of fiery wood make light shadows against the canvas as they scattered everywhere—any one of which could have served as a stake if they didn't set him alight first!

The same was true of the spindles freed by a single cannonball that smashed through the railings a second later, over and over and over again, as if batted back and forth by an unseen hand. Mircea, who had just crawled out from the other side of the sail, dove and ducked and rolled and swore. And then ripped up a heavy trapdoor to use as a shield, keeping the flying, jagged things from piercing his heart.

And had one pierce his leg, instead.

The sharp splinter slammed through his calf, causing a bright shock of pain, but less than the fire that caught in his hair a moment later. Mircea ripped off his shirt, using it to put out the flames, while desperately trying to come up with something, anything, to keep his pursuers busy. Something other than killing him!

And he found it.

Underneath the trapdoor was the deck with the cannon —and the small kegs of gunpowder used to light them. Because the humans who built this ship didn't have magic, did they? But what they did have worked pretty well, Mircea thought, jumping down and grabbing a keg, and pulling out the plug. And touching the now flaming end of his shirt to the ring of black powder around the opening, before launching it back on deck.

And into the pile of vampires who had been in the process of following him down.

Ha! Mircea thought, as the keg went off in their faces, which was good.

And sent flying, burning, exploding debris everywhere, which was bad.

Very bad, when some of it ripped through additional kegs, setting them alight, which in turn exploded and caught more, and suddenly it sounded like half the ship was going up.

But Mircea couldn't be sure.

Because he was down a couple more decks, proving just how fast a really motivated vampire could move. And was still staying just ahead of the flames, which were everywhere now. Which was probably why Jerome was staring at him in horror as he ran through the door of a cargo hold and kept on going, before realizing what he'd just seen and backing up.

"*Luridi branco di cani bastardi*!" Jerome yelled.

"What?"

"Those filthy sons of bitches! They're blowing up the ship!"

Mircea blinked at him. "Yes. Yes, they are."

And then Jerome was hitting him, which, all things considered, he couldn't really blame—

Oh.

His hair had still been on fire.

"We have a problem," Jerome yelled, shaking him.

"I'm aware of that—"

"No. Them!" And Jerome gestured at a huddled group of women, who were staring up at the ceiling, where all the screaming and yelling and running and exploding was going on, on the upper decks. And then looking back down at him and Jerome. And then a pretty redhead threw out a hand, and Mircea hit the far wall, so hard and so fast that it took him a minute to realize he'd actually gone through it.

Or, rather, his ass had.

His ass was now outside.

And he wasn't sure what he was supposed to do about that, since it was also the only reason the ship wasn't sinking as well as burning, since they were below the waterline. Which was a problem because they were coming. The women, that is. All of them. And they did not seem friendly.

"Don't they want to be rescued?" he asked Jerome, his voice a little high. And didn't get an answer because Jerome was facing the women, his hands spread out, trying an ingratiating smile.

Judging by the fact that the next time Mircea blinked,

Jerome's ass was acting as a second plug, it hadn't worked.

"Why are they doing this?" Mircea said. "Why are they—"

"I don't know, can't you do something?"

So Mircea did. Given his current state, he didn't have many options. So he initiated his original plan for getting them out of there with a whole skin.

Of course, that had involved a suitably grateful and highly cooperative group of damsels in distress, instead of a group of furies trying to kill him, but he'd sort that out later. Right now, they needed a miracle, and he just so happened to have one. Mircea pressed the stone on Hieronimo's necklace, and the huge yellow maw of the portal flashed into existence in the middle of the cramped deck, almost consuming it.

And did consume the women, who had been charging them all at once. Until they suddenly winked out of existence, followed quickly by Jerome and Mircea, wiggling painfully out of their holes and into the portal. And by an awful lot of rushing water.

"Shut it off! Shut it off!" Jerome was screaming. As what felt like the whole ocean followed them through the already terrifying ride through the portal. And back into what was now a terribly cramped and very damp back room of the bar.

"I don't... know how... to shut it off," Mircea said, slipping and sliding on the potion-slick floor, while half an ocean kept trying to drown him and people kept stepping on him and a witch kept trying to eviscerate him with something.

He didn't see what, because all he saw was searing yellow light and splashing water. But someone threw a fiery plume that evaporated a good deal of the latter a moment later, after he dodged the witch's attack. And a mage, who had been standing behind him, did not.

And went up in flames.

"You said they'd have left by now!" Jerome yelled as the fiery mage went running out the door, screaming, and ran into a crowd of others coming this way.

They seemed to have been waiting outside for the most

part, maybe because there was nothing to sit on in here, but were now flinging themselves into the fray.

And into the water, because the first man had just set them alight.

"I think they were waiting for us to come back!" Mircea yelled.

"I know they were waiting for us to come back!" Jerome shrieked, looking furious. "But you said they'd all be gone!"

"It appears I was wrong!"

"*I know you were wrong!* What do we *do now*?"

The portal cut out abruptly after dumping another ton of water on them. Which helped with the mages, who had recovered just in time to get washed off their feet again. It didn't help at all with the witches, who had braced themselves in the corners and by the counter, and were now looking daggers at Mircea. And raising some of those stick things he'd seen earlier, and which might not have been sticks, after all.

Cazzo!

The portal spiraled into being again, and Mircea jumped through, hoping Jerome would have the sense to do likewise.

He did.

Unfortunately, so did the witches, who seemed to be a good deal more persistent than their mage counterparts. Or perhaps they are just crazy, Mircea thought, as one grabbed him around the neck *while they were still sliding.* Good thing I don't need to breathe, Mircea thought, and threw her off.

And then thought it again as the portal let out—into a flooded hold, because it was almost completely underwater now. Which surprised Mircea, who thought all the water had drained down the portal. But apparently not.

And then the whole thing lurched to the side, sending a wave sloshing through the hold and Mircea slamming into a wall.

Jerome surfaced alongside him, while Mircea was still trying to blink salt water out of his eyes. "We need… to find… the witches," Jerome said, grabbing his arm. "They'll drown!"

"I don't think they're going to drown," Mircea said, staring.
"What? Why?"

"That's why!" Mircea grabbed his friend and jerked him down, just as a bolt of something blasted through the water and took out the wall behind them.

Leaving them underwater in a rapidly sinking ship full of what looked like vengeful mermaids, because the witches weren't in danger. The witches *were* the danger, having either done some sort of spell to help them breathe underwater or being really good at holding their breath. And, either way, they were coming.

Which, Mircea belatedly realized, was why he could still see, despite the fact that the portal light was now gone. Because spell fire was lighting up the water, just as it had the air outside, in bright streamers of pink and red and gold and orange. Which made it a little hard to distinguish from the fire still burning on the decks above, reflecting down through the open doorway.

The whole image was so surreal that for a moment, Mircea just stared.

And then Jerome's voice came in his head, resounding like a scream. *Snap out of it, or I swear to God I'll kill you myself!*

Mircea snapped out of it. And started swimming. And, fortunately, vampires swim really fast, because he and Jerome found themselves having to navigate a gauntlet of collapsing doorways, exploding spells, and detonating casks of gunpowder. Apparently, the latter hadn't had time to get really wet yet, or else the spells the witches were flinging were able to compensate, because they went up just fine.

And they went up everywhere. The previous explosions had blown holes in the upper decks, allowing casks and cannonballs to rain down from above, and Mircea was damned if the witches missed a single one! The force of the explosions battered him and Jerome violently as they struggled toward the surface, chased by spells, dodging falling cannon, and pierced by shards of glowing wood from every explosion, which didn't set them aflame only because they were under a few tons of water!

And all while they struggled to spot an area above where it might be safe to surface.

Jerome spied one and pointed, just before a trio of casks went off underneath them. The resulting upswell of water shot them toward the surface, and they helped by swimming as fast as they could, hoping the witches were momentarily blinded behind them. And somehow, they made it, breaking through the surface a moment later, bleeding from a few dozen wounds and staring around in terror.

At slick patches of oil still burning on the surface. At the battle going on, even fiercer now, between the remaining ships. At vampires, whose night vision could spot them even in the dark shadow of a sinking hull, and drain them, if they didn't keep their heads down.

And somehow manage not to scream.

At least, Mircea managed it. Jerome had been screaming in his head for pretty much the whole time, and didn't seem likely to stop. Until Mircea slapped him.

"W-what?" Jerome spluttered and went under again, before emerging to glare at Mircea. "What the—"

"Snap out of it, or I swear to God I'll kill you myself!"

Jerome stared at him wildly for a moment. And then he blinked. "All right," he said, swallowing. "All right, I deserved that. Now what?"

"Now we get out of here!"

"We can't get out of here without those witches!"

"The hell we can't! They want to kill us!"

"Listen to me," Jerome grabbed Mircea's shoulders. Which would have been more comforting if his gray eyes hadn't perfectly reflected the spell fire flashing everywhere. "If we don't find them, and somehow get them to Hieronimo's people, we are going to lose this war—"

"I don't care about your war! I have a daughter to think about!"

"Yes, you do. And how well do you think she's going to be treated by the rebels, if they gain control? How well will you be, as a known associate of the consul's? We already chose our side, Mircea! And now we live with it, or we die with it—and our houses."

Mircea stared at him for a moment, and then he swore. Which was cut off when something grabbed his heel from below. And jerked him down, lightning quick, like some fell monster from the deep.

But it wasn't a monster; it was a witch. And only the one. And while there had been a time when Mircea had had qualms about fighting a woman, that was before he'd seen what the women of this new world could do. They were easily a match for the men, and might be worse, if these damned witches were anything to go on!

If she wanted a fight, so be it.

He spun and jerked her up, getting a hand on her neck. And started to drain her. Only to find out in shock that she was already doing it to him.

She'd somehow acquired the skill of a vampire, and one far more powerful than he.

Mircea stared up at her as she forced him down, at her gleeful face limned by fire, at her hair turned green by some trick of the light, and despaired. He could feel the life draining out of him, and young as he was, with no family to draw from, exsanguination was a death sentence. Even if the witch didn't curse him when she was done, it wouldn't matter.

He would drift here on the water, immobilized, unknowing, unseeing, a corpse in all but name.

Until the sun came up and finished the job.

Dorina, he thought, and began thrashing about, fighting not just for himself, but for her. Jerome was right; she wouldn't survive on her own, not with only a half-blind servant to protect her. He had to get free...

But the witch was too powerful. She wasn't absorbing the blood she was pulling from him, her human body unable to use it, so it floated around them in a cloud. He tried to reabsorb it, but it was mixing with seawater and already breaking down.

What he received back wasn't a tenth of what he was losing.

And losing fast.

He wasn't going to win this.

He stared upwards, and the face above him changed, from that of a stranger to that of another girl, the one he loved most in the world. The one he'd tried so hard for, risked so much for, yet it hadn't been enough. His eyesight was fading, but still he saw her, so clearly.

"Dorina—"

His hand went out to touch her face for the last time, and his mind searched for hers, wanting her to know how he felt, for her not to blame herself. "I chose this," he whispered. "I chose..."

He felt something swell up inside him, an overwhelming surge of love and sorrow and loss, things he couldn't put into words on the best of days, and certainly not now. But he sent it to her anyway, holding nothing back, and felt it flood her mind. Felt the cheek under his hand, which had been tense and hard, soften, and turn into his touch...

And the next moment, he was being pulled to the surface, was breaking through the waves, and was staring dizzily at Jerome, who had just fought off one vampire.

And had three others coming up behind him.

Who were suddenly blown off the side of the ship and back through the air, Mircea didn't know how. Until he looked behind him, at the witch with the red hair who had cursed him halfway through a ship's hull, and then drained him almost dry. And who was now cuddling up behind him, her arms around his waist, her cheek rubbing against his back like a cat.

"What?" Jerome asked, looking from Mircea to the woman and back again. "What?"

But Mircea had no idea.

What the *hell*?

CHAPTER TWELVE

Present Day, Dory
In the back of a freaked-out cabbie's car, Paris

W hat the *hell*?" I woke up to pain, bone-deep and aching, to ringing in my ears, and to a vampire in my face.

Who was promptly thrown against some glass hard enough to shatter it. Someone screamed, something slung wildly back and forth as I leapt after the vamp, and someone grabbed my fist. And whoever had grabbed me was strong, because it took effort to continue with the plan of breaking the vamp's nose.

Successful effort, I thought, hearing it crunch.

There was more screaming after that, some rather inventive cursing, and a sudden forward and then backward motion, as whatever kind of conveyance we were in abruptly stopped. A car door opened and didn't shut. And somebody went shrieking bloody murder down the street.

"Can you handle this?" A woman asked, and got a growl back from somebody.

"Catch him!"

It was the vamp speaking, I realized. He had fangs out, and there was blood on them. My blood. I slammed my fist into his face a dozen more times in quick succession before realizing who it was I was beating up.

And then I hit him again anyway, before he snarled and threw me out of the cab, shoving me up against an old brick wall.

"Careful," someone else said.

I blinked and saw my uncle Radu sitting in the back of a cab, leaning forward to peer out at us.

"Always am," I told him, and decked Marlowe.

Or, rather, I tried. But the damned man was sturdy. It was annoying.

He caught my fist, his face swelling up nicely, and squeezed.

"Ow," I said, and saw him smile.

He was missing a tooth.

I smiled back.

And then I did deck him, because I have two hands.

There followed a tussle, which ended with me cheek to brick again, my jacket being ripped off, and my shirt torn in half.

"I have a boyfriend," I informed him, through smushed lips, and heard him mutter something.

It sounded like "not with a ten-foot pole", but I could be mistaken. The ringing in my ears had slacked off, but wasn't entirely gone. Like the pain.

I jabbed an elbow in Marlowe's direction and heard him swear. Which did not stop him from probing what was obviously an open wound. "What the hell?" I yelled and thrashed some more.

"I need more light!" he snapped, and Radu got out of the car, I assumed to come rescue me. Because my messed-up head was still trying to see two places at once, a moonlit ocean and a moonlit street, and my eyes kept crossing. It was interfering with my plan to kill Marlowe before he finished digging my spine out of my back, so some assistance would be appreciated.

But no.

Radu casually knocked over a streetlamp instead, which caused another yelp from somewhere nearby.

"How did he do that?" Some guy yelled in French. "How did he—"

"Go to sleep!" a woman said, and a moment later, somebody was snoring.

Probably the cabbie I could see through the side of my

eye, now draped over the hood of his vehicle. Oblivious to the fact that I was being manhandled by a seriously pissed-off master vamp. Or make that two, because Radu was holding the streetlamp almost in my face.

"What are you *doing*?" I demanded, because he wasn't as family-obsessed as Mircea, but he didn't usually help people assault me, either!

"This was your idea," he said mildly. "Now do hold still."

"Can you see anything? Is there anything there?" the woman's voice asked, from closer in.

"Get out of my light!" Marlowe snapped.

She got out of the light.

"Did you bite me?" I growled at Marlowe. Because there was going to be hell to pay if so.

"No! But if you don't hold still, I'll consider it."

"Then why is my blood on your fangs?"

"You scratched yourself when you belted me in the damned mouth!"

"Oh."

Okay, then.

"Is there a place called Amour?" Marlowe asked, after a moment.

"Amour?" That was the woman again, and she did not sound happy.

"You know it?"

"Yes, but... we don't usually go there."

"And why not?"

"It's run by the Pentacle."

"The what?" I asked.

"Five powerful families that control a number of illegal activities throughout Europe," she told me. "Amour is a club they use as a sort of... central meeting place. It's what the name stands for: Aurand, Macedo, Østergård, Umberger, and Razzanti. They named it after themselves. We usually leave them alone."

"You leave alone rival powers to your senate?" Marlowe demanded.

"They aren't rival powers. They have their own... areas of concern... and we have ours."

"If they're vampires in your territory, they are your concern! That's what a senate is!"

"That may be what your senate is. Anthony does things differently—"

"Yes! And where is Anthony?"

"Would somebody tell me what the hell is going on?" I demanded. Because my back hurt like hell.

And looked like it, too, when somebody held up a mirror.

It was a small compact variety, and the little alley where we'd stopped was dark, except for where the streetlight was threatening to blind me. But I somehow managed to focus anyway. And promptly freaked the hell out.

The next moment, Marlowe was being slammed against the wall, repeatedly, while the woman made startled noises, and Radu sighed.

"Best to let them get it out of their systems, my dear." He pulled her back.

"They're going to kill each other!"

"Oh, probably not."

"Don't take any bets," I snarled and threw Marlowe over the car.

The woman was the blonde from the plane. I recognized her when I tossed the streetlight after Marlowe. Elise something.

And then I hit hard cobblestones, because I swear the bastard turned in mid-air, batted the lamp away, and pounced on me, like a damned cat.

"Would you listen to me, you insane bi—"

I put a fist in his mouth because I don't like that word. I don't like having things carved into my flesh, either! "You let him do this?" I asked Radu, feeling strangely hurt.

"*You* let him do this, only he didn't do this, Louis-Cesare did," Radu said, with his usual lack of clarity.

"What?"

Marlowe, whom I had just flipped to more easily pound his

head into the ground, flipped me back. And somehow succeeded in holding me down for a minute. Mainly because I was still staring at Radu.

"Listen to me, you—" he caught himself that time. "*Will* you listen?"

"To what? What the hell—"

"Did you or did you not ask to be cursed?"

"Are you crazy? Why would I—" And then it hit me. Claude and his reconstructed spell. And then everything came flooding back, including me carving a question into my forearm, because what happened to one happened to both, right?

So I'd hoped Louis-Cesare would get the fleshy version of an email.

I held my arm up. My healing ability had already started to smudge it, but the outlines were still there. Like whatever he'd replied—on my back!

"Let me up," I told Marlowe, more calmly.

He hesitated.

"Or I'll knee you in the groin."

He let me up.

"What does it say?" I asked, taking the mirror from Elise. But between the now destroyed light and the fact that the cuts were backwards in the mirror, it was impossible to tell.

Well, for me anyway.

"How did you even think to do this?" she asked, staring at my bloody flesh.

"My uncle taught me."

She looked at Radu.

"Not that uncle."

Her eyes widened.

"Can you read it?" I asked impatiently.

"I... yes. Yes. It's Anthony's writing," she said, bending closer. And then looked up excitedly. "That must mean they're together!"

"Together where?"

She smeared some blood out of the way. "It's Louis-

Cesare's words. Anthony must be transcribing for him." Yeah, well, it's a little hard to carve up your own back. "He says he traced Anthony to Amour and then lost consciousness. He woke up in a cell with—yes! They're together!"

"I'm thrilled you're pleased," I gritted out. "Does it say *where*?"

She shook her head. "No, he doesn't know. But... but we have to find them by midnight."

"Why?"

She broke off, blinking at my back, and then up at me.

"Elise?" I growled. "Just say it!"

She swallowed. "Because that's when they plan to kill them."

"I still don't like this," Elise said, half an hour later. "We should wait until Heinrich sends help."

"You said it could be an hour," I pointed out.

We'd been on our way to see him, at his compound outside Paris, when Louis-Cesare's message arrived. Only the cab had just been meant to take us to where Elise parked her car, because it was a lengthy trip. One that I was relieved we hadn't taken, because we might not have been back in time.

"He likes to be conservative. It's probably less—"

"It doesn't matter," I told her. "After the trip back to Claude's for the outfits, we have less than two hours to finish this. What if they're not here?"

She looked unhappy. "I'm more worried about whether they are."

Marlowe muttered something, which I didn't hear because I was being cut in half.

"Damn it! I just want to cover the scars, not make them worse!" I said, as the freaking corset ate into my wounds.

"It would look better cinched tight," Radu pointed out.

"And I'll fight better if I can breathe!"

"Oh, yes. I always forget you need to do that," he murmured, but let it out a little.

His own corset was breathtakingly perfect, because of course it was. It matched the sheer, Gaultier-esque black-tinged playsuit he had on, with tight black shorts, a voluminous silk trench coat, and a top hat. Because Amour, it seemed, had a dress code.

Unfortunately for my back, that dress code seemed a little high fashion, a little goth, and a little *Rocky Horror Picture Show*. And a whole lot of pretentious twats who thought they were cooler than they were. I was going to eviscerate someone for making me wear this!

But I had to admit, it was almost worth it to see Marlowe in fishnets, which were fashionably shredded considering that Radu and Elise had had to practically sit on him to get him into them.

I didn't know what he was complaining about. His legs weren't bad, and he had the least weird getup of all, considering that he wasn't even in a corset. Just a perfectly normal tux, sleek and black and surprisingly well-fitted—including the short shorts it came with instead of trousers, hence the hose. He'd flat-out refused heels, however, leaving him in regular dress shoes, which ruined the lines, and had caused Claude to throw up his hands in disgust.

But between my corset and underwear combo, Elsie's catsuit—which I'd have fought her for, but it was more skin than lace—and Radu and Marlowe's Daisy Dukes, we were all set.

Except for one little thing.

"All right," Elise said, looking determined. "But remember what I said. We have fifteen minutes, maybe twenty. Definitely no more. And possibly less if I lose my concentration."

"I want to see it before we go in," Marlowe told her stubbornly.

"Did you not hear what I just said?" she demanded, her voice a little high. Because I was getting the impression that Elise was more the paper pusher type of op, instead of the bang-

bang version. She seemed a little... stressed. "It's exhausting. I do it now, and it shortens our time inside, and it's short enough!"

"And if it doesn't work, our time will be zero, and we'll be dead." Marlowe crossed his arms. And somehow managed to be intimidating, despite the hosiery.

"Oh, all right!" Elise whisper shrieked, making Marlowe raise an eyebrow. And then raise both of them a second later when—

"Okay," I told her. "That's seriously cool."

"Who is your master?" Marlowe murmured, watching the colors in the air above us swirl and shift and change.

"Why?"

"I'm thinking of acquiring you from him."

I caught Elise's fist because she appeared to have the same reaction to Marlowe that I did. And while I'd love another go at him, especially with help, we were running low on time. "Later," I told her.

She nodded.

From her expression, it was a promise.

"Oh, that's quite nice, isn't it?" Radu said, batting at the clouds of masters' power that were floating about, but not fighting with each other as they had on the plane. Because they were no longer from different families.

Somehow, Elise had wreathed all three vamps in the same slightly effeminate pink haze.

"Don't let it fool you," she told us. "Razzanti is... formidable. But they're the least well-known here, rarely leaving their own compound outside Florence." She glanced at Marlowe. "Do you speak Italian?"

He looked vaguely annoyed. "Some."

"Some won't work. Just stay—"

"Why? This is Paris."

"But we're supposed to be Italian!"

"Look down your nose at them, say their accent is terrible, and that you'd rather speak their language than have them butcher yours."

"What?"

"It's what the French do."

She pinched her nose. "Just... stay to the back, and keep quiet."

He looked like he was going to say something else, but she didn't give him a chance. "How about you?" she asked Radu.

Who promptly told her how beautiful she was in fluent Italian, and how much he liked her shoes.

She smiled at him. Because women always smiled at the men of our family. Well, except for Drac.

They'd only smiled at him when he went away.

Sort of like Marlowe.

"You said we were in a hurry?" he reminded her.

She ignored him. "And you?" she asked me.

"Certo."

"Va bene. You'll go in front with me. Razzanti is led by women; no one should find it odd if I do the talking. Try to stay in front of the men as much as possible. Your uncle, while charming, is often in Paris—"

"And Marlowe is Marlowe."

She nodded. "Someone may recognize him, but we'll have to take that chance."

"Tick tock," the man himself reminded us. "Or should I say that in Italian, too?"

"You shouldn't say anything!" she said viciously. "We'll do the talking!"

And with that, we were off.

CHAPTER THIRTEEN

Present Day, Dory
Amour, Paris

T he nightclub/command center of the Pentacle was hard to miss. Unlike most underground operations, which tried to slink around the edges of society and stay in the dark, Amour was bright, loud, and in-your-face. And that was before we even got in the door.

We rounded the corner from the next block, where we'd left the cabbie snoring behind his wheel, and were confronted by three eighteenth-century buildings that had been gutted and turned into one. I stared at them, wondering if this was a case of hiding in plain sight. Because the large, neoclassical façade was practically vibrating from the music throbbing inside, and was painting the buildings opposite with neon flashes and huge, leaping shadows.

There were two guys at the double doors, I noticed, as we picked our way across the street. Big bruisers in tuxedos, standing at the top of an expansive set of stairs, and strobed by multicolored flashes and a blast of sound every time the doors opened. Which was constantly, with a steady stream of people moving inside from the crush on the steps, while being replaced by more from a long line of shiny black cars stretching the length of the street.

It looked like a damned red carpet.

But nobody, as far as I could tell, was being relieved of hardware, even though many were wearing weapon-like accessories, or were trailed by bodyguards bristling with them.

But the door guys never even blinked. Until a couple of clueless and fairly astonished-looking tourists tried to get in, and were velvet roped right the hell out of there.

This, it seemed, was a private party.

Good, I thought, and hoisted one of Claude's signature cloth bags further onto my shoulder. It was serving as a replacement for my leather jacket, which in turn had been serving as a replacement for my duffel bag of nasty tricks. It would have made it through customs all right, with the right wards, but might have gotten rerouted to Tijuana, so it had had to stay home. And I had clinked through security without so much as a raised eyebrow, thanks to a witch I know.

And would hopefully clink through the front door here as well, despite the skimpy outfit, because weapons seemed to be not only tolerated but expected.

A shame these are the bad guys, I thought.

It was my kind of place.

Well, except for the fashion.

"Is this a costume party?" I asked Elise, watching a couple in what could only be described as eighteenth-century drag, head up the stairs. The outfits were black and blood red, the stacked heels were maybe a foot tall, the faces were powdered and littered with sparkly little beauty marks, the legs were bare except for silk thigh highs, and the pompadours were high—on both sexes.

I suddenly felt seriously underdressed. Like a sad, brown wren in comparison to a couple of blinged-out peacocks. Maybe I should have listened to Claude and gone with the goth wedding gown, I thought, watching a woman in a similar ensemble laugh with a guy in a sparkly black unitard. And then sweep inside on the heels of a woman in a playsuit studded with a few thousand sharp, silver-tipped spikes.

Elise didn't say anything.

I looked up to find her staring around, biting her lip. Her hair was currently pink, from the latest splash of color, and half her face was green. But it was the expression that worried me.

She looked gobsmacked.

Like maybe this wasn't what she'd expected, either.

"Elise?" No response. "Elise!"

She blinked that time, and her head jerked around. She was already taller than me—no surprise, most people are. But the shiny black stilettos Claude had provided put her blonde head a foot above mine. Which might explain why she didn't look at me, but above me.

Or there may have been another reason.

I turned to see a freaking palanquin being carted up the stairs by four burly human types in little leather skirts and Greek sandals. And reclining on the silken pillows within was a creature in pure white silk, except for where it was splashed by the ever-changing colors. Including a white veil, just sheer enough to make out the perfect masculine features inside.

It was complete theatre, and weird as hell, but I didn't get a chance to enjoy it.

Because the next second, I was being jerked around to face the other way. Where a guy in a black speedo and a black-and-white checked fur with a train so long it rippled down the entire flight of stairs was passing by. Only, I guess he wasn't the point.

But something sure was.

Because Elise was about to leave an imprint of her hand permanently embedded into my arm.

"What is the problem?" Marlowe hissed, joining us.

I guess he'd noticed her expression, too.

Elise didn't answer.

"Are they always so brazen?" I asked, trying to knock her out of whatever the hell. And because I just couldn't get over it. I'd expected a small, dark venue, filled with shifty-looking types, not whatever this was.

It looked like a paranormal circus, and that was before the guy with the black leopard got out of a car.

"And so distinguished?" Radu murmured. "I've already seen two senators."

"Where?" Marlowe said sharply.

I couldn't blame him for overlooking them, super spy or not, because there was so damned much to see. But once you did notice, they were hard to miss. Radu nodded at the other side of the half mile of stairs, at a dark-haired beauty dressed in what was mostly a bunch of thin, black silk strands hanging from a jeweled collar, surrounded by a crowd of sycophants, also in black. Marlowe's eyes narrowed.

And then flicked up the stairs to where another woman was standing, also in the midst of a retinue. She was a tall redhead wearing a mass of crimson veils so sheer and so light that they shifted on every breeze. Making her look like she was wearing a bunch of red smoke.

Her coterie was a bunch of tall, willowy types, with model pretty faces, if you didn't count the fangs. But they were dressed in columns of plain scarlet, I guess so they didn't draw attention from the boss. They were standing around, posing like they were waiting for the *Vogue* photographer to show up.

"Jaqueline and Aagtje," Marlowe said, with a tone I hadn't heard from him before. Almost wary.

"And Heinrich," Elise said, finally finding her voice. And sounding strangled.

"What?" That was me, trying to keep up.

"Where?" Marlowe snapped. And then answered his own question when his eyes fixed on the vision in white. The elegant profile had turned to watch us as he was carried through the front doors, causing Marlowe to curse. And then to show off his vocabulary again at the sight of a squad of leather-clad guards —in black, of course—with bared arms and bared weapons, heading our way. They looked like the fashion police, in their overly styled outfits, but the power radiating off them wasn't funny.

"Go dim," Marlowe snapped, and Radu threw the trench over the still stunned-looking woman, and then the two of them
—

Disappeared.

Master powers, I thought enviously, and then Marlowe

threw out a hand, demonstrating his own. The first four guards were suddenly a lot flatter, and went smashing back into the pack—or the ones who had made it through the door, anyway. But there were about a hundred more behind them, and while Marlowe was good, I didn't think he was that good.

"Run?" I offered.

"Run!"

And then we were pelting off the side of the stairs, knocking Senator Red Smoke into the bushes along with half her ladies. And I guess they weren't used to that sort of hoodlum behavior at the illustrious European court, because it caused quite a stir among the well-dressed crowd. Or maybe that was the power bombs Marlowe kept throwing behind us, spilling guards down the now-cracked steps half a dozen at a time.

People were screaming, more were running, and somebody in the bushes below wrapped a hand around my ankle, trying to drain me.

I looked down at the well-dressed senator and put a stiletto heel through her perfectly made-up face. And then left it there, when Marlowe grabbed my arm, jerking me away. Probably because of the hundred or so more guards coming at us from around the building.

So we went up—somehow. It happened so fast, it felt like Marlowe scaled the side of the building like Spiderman. What I guess actually happened was something less Marvel-iscious: he used the decent-sized gaps between the large stone blocks as grips for his feet and free hand, and dragged me up with the other.

I could have helped, but frankly, it would have been slower. And right now slow was dead. Because Marlowe wasn't the only one who could climb.

I felt a hand grab me before we even reached the roof, and I kicked out viciously, losing my other shoe and sending someone I didn't even see sailing back into the night. And then we were up and running, tearing across the roof and sliding through an open dormer window, into a small, dark room. And then fleeing from there into a tight hallway and down some stairs, before running into a bunch of people who looked at us in surprise.

And then surged past us to attack the guards on our heels, *en masse*, while Marlowe and I just stared at each other.

"Razzanti," Marlowe said, as the clash turned into an all-out brawl. And I suddenly realized that I could see a faint pink cloud around our rescuers, if I squinted.

Thank you, Elise, I thought fervently. And then we were moving again, before our defenders figured out we were fakes. Down another hall and through a series of tiny rooms, where we finally came to rest—

Somewhere. Everything had happened so fast that it felt like my brain was trying to keep up with my eyes. But when it finally managed it, I realized that we were in a closet.

And that Marlowe was talking to somebody.

The silent grimacing of a vamp phone call seemed to go on forever, although it was probably just a few seconds. But vampires could cover a lot of ground in a few seconds. I poked him.

"Radu," he told me briefly.

"Are they—"

"They're all right. And they're in. On the main floor." He listened some more, and the scowl he'd started with grew exponentially. "Where a giant-sized screen is showing another party," he told me grimly. "One taking place at our senate in New York."

"What?" I stared at him. "Why would they—"

But Marlowe wasn't listening. Marlowe was cursing in a vicious undertone, at me, at Radu, at himself—I wasn't sure. But the vocabulary was frankly astounding. As was the passion.

"I should have known!" he told somebody. And then he cursed some more.

"Should have known what?"

"The Pythia warned me—"

"What Pythia? That weird seer?" He still wasn't listening, so I grabbed him. "Marlowe! If you don't start making sense—"

"The Pythia warned me that I either retrieve Anthony, or our consul would also die," he told me harshly. "That's why I'm here, instead of in New York. That's why I broke away in the middle of some extremely delicate negotiations to come here myself. I couldn't trust another operative with this—"

"Trust them with *what*? What are you—"

"The Pythia couldn't tell me that. She just said that Anthony's fate was linked to the consul's—our consul's. But now we know, don't we?"

"We do?" I said, still lost.

Until he spelled it out for me.

"This isn't just an attack. It's a *coup*. They're going to take Anthony out at midnight, and thereby also kill our consul, his twin—"

"—because what happens to one happens to both." I stared at him, finally getting it. "You think they have the full spell."

"Heinrich is Anthony's spymaster. Of course, he'd have shared it with him!"

"And now they're going to show the deaths on the big screen, to let everyone know there's a new power in town."

He nodded. "And not just here. If the consul dies in front of the leaders of the other senates—" He cursed, and broke off. Because yeah, I didn't know what that would do, either.

Start the biggest free-for-all in the world, over who would replace her? Completely derail the war effort into a bunch of next-level power plays? Cause ambitious senators in other courts to try and take down their leaders as well? All of the above?

Because, with two consuls suddenly dead, and a major war looming, anything could happen, anything at all.

And none of it good.

"You have to have operatives here," I said.

"Yes, but not enough. The consul is allied with Anthony. We depend on his people when we have business here—"

"And his people are dirty as fuck."

"At least some of them—"

"But maybe not all of them! Can you—"

But Marlowe was already shaking his head. "Anthony surrounded himself with sycophants and yes-men—and women. Anyone with the power to challenge him, he used Louis-Cesare to intimidate and sideline."

"And now it's catching up with him."

Marlowe nodded. "The senators Heinrich—damn his eyes! —hasn't suborned, he's doubtless controlled, or he wouldn't risk this. And they're too damned weak to help us in any case."

"But you must have somebody! The time for an undercover op is long past, Marlowe!"

"You think I don't know that?" he glared at me. "I have people coming from our office in Brussels—it's closest. And others from London and Frankfurt. But by the time they get here —"

"Louis-Cesare will be dead." Because no way did they kill Anthony and keep him alive. I didn't know why he wasn't dead already. But the painful ridges on my flesh testified to his continued existence.

Maybe they wanted the spectacle of killing Anthony with his old protector at his side, I thought. Rub in the enormity of his defeat. Or maybe Louis-Cesare had racked up a few enemies of his own over the years, keeping his bastard of a consul in power. Damn it, if they didn't kill Anthony, I was going to do it myself!

If I could find him.

"Radu thinks they may be in the basement," Marlowe said, his brow furrowing as Radu re-established contact. "They're not letting anybody down there, and despite the search for us, they just added more guards to the vestibule." His mouth twisted grimly. "And the door. And the stairs."

"Thank you, Heinrich," I said, and unshouldered my pack.

Marlowe grabbed my arm. "He's an idiot. That doesn't mean he isn't dangerous."

"So am I."

"Not for long. You didn't have Claude take off the spell—"

"No."

"Why?"

I looked up at him because I couldn't see why he cared. If we didn't get to them by midnight, this was over anyway. "I couldn't know if Louis-Cesare was here or being held somewhere nearby, and the spell gets stronger the closer we get. I needed it."

"But if Louis-Cesare dies at midnight, so do you!"

"He isn't going to die," I said, and opened my pack. Because, unlike Marlowe and every freaking other person in my life, I don't have sparkly master powers. What I do have is serious firepower and a lot of dirty tricks. And the experience to use them.

Marlowe looked in the bag, and his mouth twisted. But this time, it looked grimly amused. "Finally, some goddamned Basarab ruthlessness."

"They threw a party," I told him, pulling out a Glock. "So let's party."

CHAPTER FOURTEEN

Present Day, Dory
Various levels of Amour, Paris

There are many ways to reach the lowest level of a building. Elevators, stairs, or perhaps a leisurely stroll outside, to see if there's a basement entrance.

Or, you know, you could do it our way.

"Shiiiiiiiit!" Marlowe yelled as we fell through the hole that my acid bomb had just burned into the floor, and promptly hit another. Floor, that is. With our faces. And then had to immediately flip to either side, because somebody was shooting at us through the newly made hole above.

I returned fire while trying to avoid the acid that was still burning around the edges of the piece of flooring we'd ridden down on top of. And which was now eating through to the next floor as well. Which turned out to be a good thing, because a knot of guards had just run in the door.

And fell through the newly made hole.

We jumped through after them a second later, because our erstwhile family had caught up with us, and they didn't look happy.

"Auggghhh!" That was me, falling on top of Marlowe, who had fallen on top of some of the guards.

I rolled off just before some more hit down and made a Marlowe sandwich. And then grabbed my gun and fired up into the hole, where a bunch of Razzanti family members were trying to fire back, only they kept getting in the way of my bullets.

Some more guards ran in from the hall, a larger number

this time. Too large, so I hit 'em with a love bomb. Which made them stop fighting and start doing other things for a moment, which was fun but not all that helpful. Because I didn't have another for the Razzantis.

So I reloaded a clip, emptied that one too, and then scrambled back onto the train—

And practically bit through my tongue when we hit down on floor number three.

Fortunately, Marlowe had dispatched the men who had ended up as the bread to his sandwich. Unfortunately, that didn't help much, because we'd just slammed into the main floor. At least, I assumed that was why the drop had been so damned long—the ballroom had triple-height ceilings, an expansive dance floor, and an IMEX-sized screen showing another party.

And a crowd of wanna-be cool kids, who were mostly interested in getting out of our way.

Good for them, I thought.

And not so good for us, because it left a clear path for approximately five hundred guards to stampede at us.

"Why did it stop?" Marlowe asked, smacking the terrazzo flooring. And, I assumed, talking about the bomb residue.

"It didn't," I told him. "Terrazzo's just hard!"

And then my searching hand came up with a shiny, shiny dislocator. Which I held up, and the stampede slammed to a halt—or maybe a pile would be more precise. Because the ones in back hit the ones in front, who had just stopped dead and who thus ended up sprawled on the floor. And stayed there, because they liked their body parts where they were, instead of distributed randomly around their persons.

Or onto other persons who might be near them; the spell was versatile.

Like the well-armed guests, who were suddenly dropping champagne glasses for weapons.

"Why isn't it working?" Marlowe yelled, stomping on the floor.

And I guess he stomped hard. Because a second later, it fell out from under us, just as a bunch of bullets and knives flew over us. And I made the juddering acquaintance of floor number four.

I'd gotten knocked on my ass by the fall, and I lay there for half a sec, looking back up into the hole. And wondering if the guests were taking into account the fact that we'd just been standing in the middle of the floor. Meaning that, once we left, they were basically shooting at each other.

Guess not, I thought, hearing Armageddon break out upstairs.

Of course, things weren't looking so much better down here.

Because we'd come in behind the stairway full of guards, who luckily were all facing the other way. Of course, said luck only bought us a second or so, because a large amount of terrazzo flooring collapsing behind you isn't silent. Shit, I thought, and opened fire.

The problem with vamps and guns, however, is that they basically don't care. Not that it doesn't hurt, but it hurts the way a bee sting hurts a human: unpleasant, but it doesn't really put you on your ass. But that did, I thought, as Marlowe used his super special master power to explode a few heads.

That might have been enough to make the guys behind the leaders rethink their lives, except for the unfortunate fact that everybody now knew where we were. Which meant that the entire staircase full of vamps was trying to push their way into the room, forcing the guys in front to stumble at us. Which worked okay for a second or so, since the people now shooting at us through the hole in the ceiling hit them instead.

And they must have been using some high-powered ammo, because, yeah.

I guess "bee sting" wasn't really the word, I thought, looking at a guy with a suddenly split face—and head.

It had been cleaved straight down the middle, but it wasn't stopping him. Because he was a vamp, and there's only so many ways to actually kill one of them. But it screwed the hell out of his peripheral vision, which was probably why the bullets he was spraying hit a lamp, a pool table, and a sofa, but managed to avoid hitting me.

Mostly, I thought, as one of them tore through my calf.

I was a little too busy to do anything about it, however, other than to stick a knife in his least floppy eye once he ran out of ammo, because I was busy looking for something. Or, to be more precise, someone. Only that wasn't working out too well.

"Where the hell are they?" I yelled at Marlowe, who was sending power blasts through the hole in the ceiling and at the staircase, alternately.

That didn't look like it was fun, judging by the bulging neck veins and red face he turned on me. *"How the hell should I know?"*

Great.

"Midas Touch!" I yelled at the stair guys. Who had started to get organized into a stampede of their own, but who suddenly started turning and fighting back at the guys behind them. And they were fighting hard.

I almost hated to do it to them, not least because the damned potion bomb was super expensive. But you had to love craftsmanship, I thought as it exploded over some guys in the middle of the staircase. Who were trying to divest themselves of spare change, but weren't fast enough.

And a narrow stairwell is no place to be caught with suddenly animated money that starts whizzing around at about a thousand miles per hour.

Of course, it tore a lot of small holes in the walls, but it tore even more in the tightly packed vamps, the coins ricocheting over and over and over and over, and the vamps cursing and yelling and then screaming as they began to look more and more like Swiss cheese. It wouldn't kill them, of course—coins aren't made out of wood—but it cut down on the eagerness of the pursuit by, oh, a whole lot.

But there'd be others, and Marlowe was getting visibly tired. Even worse, there were no doors out of here. Which made no sense, because the buildings above were huge! There should have been an equally huge basement, not this one little room. So our people had to be here somewhere, but I didn't see—

"Goddamnit!" I swore, as something that felt like a knife tore into my arm.

Because it was a knife, I realized, but not one wielded by an attacker. Small, shallow letters were appearing along my unmarked forearm. Which might not have been legible except for the blood welling up, coloring them before it flooded them, so I had to read fast.

And then turn and scramble for the wall opposite the stairs, and run my hands over the plaster, but not find anything. And then try to punch through, which only got me a pair of bloody knuckles, and views of the hard bricks behind the pretty covering. And then somebody started carving up my ass.

"Really?" I yelled at the wall, because I had other body parts available. And I couldn't read my own ass.

"What are you doing?" Marlowe yelled.

"Read my ass!"

"What?"

"Just do it!" I stuck it out at him, "What does it say?"

He threw another invisible blow up the hole in the ceiling, where people were trying to crawl in now. And bent over. "They're behind a ward—"

"I know they're behind a ward!"

"The trigger is… I can't see." He wiped some blood.

"Marlowe, I swear to God—"

"It's in a lamp. A lamp!"

We both looked wildly around for a lamp. But most of the lights were recessed and built into the ceiling. Except for a hanging thing above the pool table, which did nothing, and a standing light near a chair, which did nothing, and a small thing on a built-in bookshelf that did nothing except serve as a cudgel for a vamp, because they were in the room now. And Marlowe was literally fighting for our lives and couldn't help, and I was about to be, too, and then—

And then I stepped on something that crunched under my heel, and hurt like a bitch.

Because it was made out of porcelain.

The shattered lamp from earlier! The one Split Face had hit because he couldn't see straight! I grabbed it, smacked a vamp in the face with it, and then jabbed at him with the jagged ends while trying to find something, anything, that might trigger a ward. But it looked like a plain old lamp to me, just like the others.

And then I realized there might be a reason for that when I spotted a final lamp across the room on a table near the stairs. But there was no way to reach it now, with guys falling through the ceiling all the time, and Marlowe's punches starting to lack oomph. And there are only so many potions you can throw when your assailants are right on top of you.

My back hit brick, after a belt from a fist I never even saw coming, and Marlowe wasn't doing much better. A vamp lunged at me, fangs glistening, and I lashed out with what I had in my hand—the lamp. Which was fairly useless, but I only needed a second to get my hand on a gun.

I didn't get it.

Because the slash across the vamp's face didn't buy me much time, but it did do something. The lamp started glowing, I guess because the switch had been hit, only no. Because the chord was dangling down by my leg. But it was suddenly getting brighter in here anyway.

Really bright.

Blindingly bright!

And then I fell backwards, onto my abused ass.

Inside the wall.

"Turn it off! Turn it off!" Someone was yelling, which would have been easy, except I was on my back with a vamp in my face. I threw him off—into Marlowe, who had just run through the wall. And who grabbed him and used him as a fleshy club, slamming him over and over and over against the other vamps now trying to pour through the wall.

Because the ward was still open!

I grabbed the lamp, and a vamp grabbed me at the same time. He jerked me back, causing me to lose my bloody grip on the slick porcelain. The lamp went bouncing, and I went sliding, and then somebody stamped a foot through the guy's brain.

Marlowe.

"Get the damned lamp!"

Blood had splattered into my face; I couldn't see. But I knew where it was, and after a second that felt like a year, my searching hands found it. And switched it off, my breath coming fast, my heart pounding.

And then pounding some more when it stubbornly continued to glow.

"Turn it off! Turn it off!"

I couldn't tell who was yelling at me, because I couldn't see. But right then, I didn't care. I just cared that flicking that little switch over and over wasn't doing shit!

"Turn it off!"

"It won't turn off!"

"Then destroy it!"

Okay, that I could do.

I stood up, grabbed a gun, and wiped blood out of my eyes. And let loose. The light flickered and went out, the ward slammed shut, leaving various vamps in various pieces, when they were caught in the suddenly-there-again wall, and somebody grabbed my arm.

Probably because I was still firing.

"Dory!"

"Augggghhhhh!"

"Dory!"

It was Marlowe, I realized, but only when I finished emptying the clip.

"What?" I turned on him. And found him grinning like the freaking madman he is. *"What?"*

"We're in."

CHAPTER FIFTEEN

1457, Mircea/Present Day Dory
Still in the Lagoon, Venice, Italy/Amour

There were only now beginning to be lamps lit in some of the houses on shore, as a sleepy populace awoke to the fact that there might be something wrong. Mircea himself was very aware of that fact, considering he was still in a burning ship, still had a group of vampires searching for him, still had a bunch of witches to round up—and still had no damned idea what was going on! Until Jerome gave him one.

It wasn't on purpose. Jerome had spoken the truth about being a spy, not a soldier. He reacted when someone attacked him, but he didn't engage himself, and seemed to lack even basic awareness of his surroundings. Which is why he hadn't seen the vampires coming up behind him before, and why he didn't notice the witch taking aim at him now.

She was on the other end of the ship, on one of the few pieces still protruding from the water, wet, bedraggled, and obviously furious. And had just pulled one of those strange, sticklike weapons from under her equally sodden cloak, obviously intending to blow the small blond to kingdom come. And while Mircea had a defender, she was plastered to his back like a very large, very friendly cat, and the few words she'd spoken weren't in a language he knew.

So he pushed Jerome underwater and threw out a hand, desperately trying to drain the witch, or at least slow her down.

What happened was... not that.

One minute, she was painting the air with a whip made

out of pure flame, about to send a storm of fire their way. And the next, she was flying backwards off her perch, the light dying as she rapidly switched her focus to a shield instead. One that was currently a half-moon of burning orange flames from a spell that hadn't come from her, and that only went out when she hit the water, well beyond the farthest ship.

Mircea looked behind him, expecting to see "his" witch laughing in victory. Instead, she was now attempting to braid his hair, which was disturbing—and was unarmed, which was more so. Because, if she hadn't spelled that witch, who had?

Mircea scanned the dark sea behind them, but there was no one there. Their ship was on one end of the little cluster of masts, with none behind it. There was nowhere for anyone to hide.

"H-how?" Jerome said, surfacing, spitting water, and almost choking, because he was trying to talk at the same time. "H-how?"

"How what?" Mircea said, only half listening. Because his head was reeling and his fingertips... felt odd. Very odd. Tingly and strangely heavy, and almost... fiery.

He quickly stuck them in the water, half expecting them to combust. Instead, they remained just fingers, ghostly white under the dark surface of the ocean, and wiggling about a bit, as if they were confused, too. He swallowed and looked up at Jerome.

"How what?" he repeated, only this time, it sounded as bewildered as he felt.

"How did you curse that witch?"

"I didn't?" But it came out more as a question.

"Don't lie! I saw. Even underwater, I *saw*!"

Yes, it had been rather hard to miss, Mircea thought. But he didn't answer, because he didn't have one. He felt dizzy.

And then Jerome grabbed him. "Think, man! It's important!"

And, yes, it was, only Mircea didn't know how he'd done it. Or even if he had. There were spells streaking about everywhere now, as the fight intensified. And as Hieronimo's men were driven back toward the shore.

They were losing, Mircea realized. Of course they were. No matter how good they might be, they had one kind of magic, while their opponents had two. It was the same reason the consul's forces were losing in his homeland. And were going to continue to do so unless something changed.

Something soon.

Mircea spied a piece of wood, part of a broken mast by the look of it, jutting above the waves, and thrust out a hand. And saw it leap out of the water and shoot across the heavens, still burning. Like a falling star in reverse.

He blinked, looking from it to his hand and back again.

The tingling was back, he thought vaguely.

And so was the shaking.

"I knew it!" Jerome yelled. "I knew it!"

And then a whole group of vampires jumped them, because of course they did. Mircea had just sent up a fiery signal, and Jerome was screaming his head off. But, while Mircea's witch might not have understood or cared about a distant threat to Jerome, she was a snarling wildcat when it came to protecting Mircea himself.

Who didn't need it because he had magical powers, too.

Only, suddenly, he didn't.

Mircea watched the witch turn on the vampires, who might have had her abilities but lacked her know-how. And reduce them to floating cinders in the time it took to blink, some still with a shocked look on what remained of their features. And, suddenly, things came together.

The witch went back to cuddling up behind him, and Mircea snapped his fingers.

And then quickly plunged them underwater, before he self-immolated, because a flame had just appeared in the air above them.

He floated there for a moment, slowly treading water.

"Mircea?" Jerome said after a moment, looking concerned.

"We need to find more witches," Mircea told him.

"Uh, yes, we do, but... how do we keep them from killing us?"

Mircea looked at his friend and felt an odd smile spread across his features. "I don't think that's going to be a problem."

◆ ◆ ◆

I came around slowly, sluggishly. Like this had happened once too often lately, and my body was starting to rebel. My limbs felt like noodles, my eyes kept trying to cross, and my hearing was wobbling around, as if a toddler was messing with a TV remote. But then I saw a foot—

Just a foot.

But a very familiar one.

I sat up abruptly, drawing in a lungful of air, preparing to scream—

Only to notice a couple of things: nobody was attacking us anymore, and the foot wasn't disembodied, as I'd first thought. Just pale, so much so that it was almost the same color as the tile it rested on, allowing the dried blood around the ankle to stand out sharply. And to give the optical illusion that it wasn't still attached to the leg behind it—the one connected to the rest of my boyfriend, who was naked and bloody and sprawled in some sort of cell. And alive!

A second later, I was getting my nose fried as I tried to press it to something that definitely wasn't glass.

"Don't touch the damned ward!" Marlowe said, as I was blown back on my ass, clutching my face. And still grinning stupidly.

Louis-Cesare grinned back, but barely. He looked as bad as I'd ever seen him, the usually glorious auburn hair straggling around a pinched, exhausted face, the blue eyes shadowed by heavy circles. I knew the feeling.

I crawled back over to the ward, but stopped just short. "Are you all right?" I asked, and heard my voice echo weirdly.

Because we were in some kind of big room I didn't care about right now. I only cared about him.

"Oh, fine, I assure you, thanks for asking," someone said who was not Louis-Cesare.

I glanced over to Louis-Cesare's right, where Anthony, also starkers, was sitting by the same brick wall. No wonder Claude's spell hadn't worked, I thought. It was designed for use with clothes, and somebody had taken all of theirs.

"Well?" Anthony said, expectantly.

"Well, what?"

"Are you not pleased to find me alive?" It was pure patrician pique that I hadn't immediately started fawning all over him.

I frowned. "I guess?"

He gave me a purely evil look. "I suppose I should be grateful to have been kidnapped along with your lover!"

"Yeah. You should." I sure as hell hadn't taken the acid express for him. "What's going on?" I asked Marlowe. "Why can't you get them out?"

He shot me a look only slightly less intense than Anthony's. He was fiddling with something in a box on the wall, something that caused him to jerk his hand back abruptly. "I'm talking to your uncle. He's walking me through this." He scowled at the air above his head. "Or he would be, if he knew what the hell he was doing!"

"Why not just get him down here?"

"Oh, what an excellent suggestion. That's why!" He flung out a hand at something behind me, and—

Well, shit.

The ward was transparent on this side, giving me a perfect view of the room beyond. Or it would have, except that it was packed—shoulder to shoulder to yet another shoulder—with vamps. There must have been three, four hundred guys out there, jammed together like sardines or people who no longer needed to breathe. And that was just in the part I could see, wedged between the walls and crowding what was left of the stairs.

Most of them were guards, judging by the outfits, but a small knot near the door was not. There was the female senator in red, Heinrich—sans veil but with a steadily flushing face—and a couple of guys in black—

And a very familiar blond.

"Jonathan," I said, and I swear the cold-eyed bastard looked up, as if he'd heard me, despite the fact that I couldn't hear anything from outside. Although I probably wouldn't have been able to anyway, over the sudden rushing in my ears.

"Grab her!" That was Louis-Cesare, his voice hoarse and barely there, thanks to whatever that creep had done to him this time.

For the last time, I thought, and snatched up my pack—

And then had somebody grab my arm, before I could decide what the most painful way would be for him to die.

"Let me go!"

"So you can what?" Marlowe demanded. "Let them in?"

"They're coming in anyway! Get the damned force field down, and we'll take them—"

"All five hundred? And likely twice that many upstairs?"

"Yes! We have three first-level masters—"

"And they have three. And two of ours are out of commission, and our resident dhampir is... at less than her best."

I stared at him, caught off guard, because that hadn't been a yell or a curse or any of his usual bluster. It had been a cold, calculated tone that somehow made it just that much clearer how bad this was. "What do you mean, out of commission?"

"He means they drained us," Anthony said. "The one you call Jonathan obtained that pernicious spell from my so-loyal security chief, but spells are like anything else: they have ranges. And my significant other is halfway around the world."

"They'd have killed him a week ago, otherwise," Marlowe said, nodding at Anthony. "But while they had the spell, they didn't have enough magic to fuel it that far. Heinrich pulled the trigger and snatched Anthony before Jonathan was ready."

"Told him I planned to go back to the U.S. early, due to a request from my lady." Anthony grimaced. "He didn't like that."

"So they had to finish gathering the magic while they sat on him," Marlowe continued. "It was a risk, but less so than having the spell not be strong enough to take out the consul."

"Otherwise, she might realize that someone was attacking her," I said, catching up. "And come after them."

"And when her life is on the line, well." Anthony smiled slightly. "Scorched earth doesn't really do it justice."

"We'd have burned the fucking city to the ground to find them!" Marlowe agreed, which made Anthony roll his eyes.

"Still so loyal. How touching."

"She deserves it, unlike some others!"

"If you mean me, why not just say so?"

"I thought I just did!"

"Can we talk about this later, like after the force field is down?" I asked, a little tightly. Because the guys outside were obviously working on the same thing, and if they managed it before we did—

I didn't think it would be good if they managed it before we did.

I guess Marlowe didn't either because he went back to work. I looked at Louis-Cesare, who had his eyes closed and his head resting back against the bricks. He hadn't contributed to the conversation at all, and considering how... vocal... he could be, that was worrying.

"They drained you repeatedly, didn't they?" I asked Anthony.

"All week. While they were preparing for their damned party. From what Louis tells me, that's Jonathan's *modus operandi*."

"Yeah." I stared at Louis-Cesare, who had been caught and tortured by this son of a bitch twice before, once for months. Jonathan had drained him over and over again, stripping him of magic and of life, while gorging himself. Each night his victim had died, only to be reborn the next day.

Just to go through it all over again.

I felt my fist clench. I didn't care what else happened tonight, I decided. Just so long as Louis-Cesare lived and Jonathan died.

And died screaming.

Anthony was talking again, because he never shut up. Something about how he'd tried to communicate with his people, but was drained so low he couldn't. Drained so low he couldn't even pull power from his family, the same way Mircea had been once, when Radu had had to manually feed him power-laced blood because he could no longer do it himself. And how the shield around the cells had also interfered with mental communication.

"Cells?" I said.

And then I realized that there was another cell. It was about the same size as the invisible box that surrounded Louis-Cesare and Anthony, but on the other end of the room. And crowded with vampires.

There were dozens of them in there, all looking a little crazed, which was how I'd noticed them. They weren't saying anything, but they kept bumping into the ward every few moments. And the *sizzle, sizzle, sizzle* was noticeable.

For a second, I got excited, thinking we had backup.

And then one of them started to cry.

He was the latest to hit the ward, but he hadn't been pushed into it like the others, by a stray elbow or knee. He'd done it on purpose, crashing into the surface, and then staying there, clawing at the invisible mass and sobbing. More desperate to get out than he was afraid of the not-inconsiderable pain.

"What are they doing here?" I asked Anthony, feeling a weird sense of deja vu.

"Oh, them." Anthony shrugged. "Lab rats. Heinrich's group changed a bunch of locals and dragged them in here to test out the spell. Had to be sure it worked."

"Locals?" I looked at them, and sure enough, there were

young and old, wealthy and poor, chic and tacky tourists all equally represented. With most of the desperate, frightened people clinging to their significant others, because of course. Heinrich hadn't cared who they were, just that they were paired up.

"They're babies; they can't help us," Anthony said, sounding dismissive. And annoyed that I wasn't paying attention.

And I wasn't. I was seeing another closed, confined space, another group of clueless baby vamps, and me, sitting on the floor, wondering why Dorina would cage them up like that.

Now, I knew. Or I knew that her better-than-average mental powers had allowed her to glimpse something of what was going on. She'd known Louis-Cesare was in trouble before I did, but our communication was also in its infancy, so she couldn't just tell me. So she'd done... what, exactly?

Kidnapped a bunch of babies and shoved them in a closet, and then sent me a series of crazy visions she'd yanked from Mircea's head. None of which I'd understood until the spell showed up, and even then... I didn't get it. I still didn't. I didn't understand what she so badly wanted to tell me.

But I would.

I looked around, but there was nothing except cold tile. Fortunately, I trained my body a long time ago not to need feather pillows and silken duvets. I lay down on the tile with my pack under my head and closed my eyes.

"What the hell are you doing?" Anthony demanded. "Kit! What is she doing?"

"Taking a nap."

CHAPTER SIXTEEN

1457, Mircea/Present Day Dory
Still burning in the Lagoon, Venice, Italy/Amour

It was easy to tell the two warring groups apart, Mircea thought. Hieronimo's mages were dark, darting shapes among the blazing hulls, able to pass through the flames while shielded without danger. The vampires, on the other hand, had been avoiding the fire from the start, which is why they'd used magic to throw it at him. They'd acquired shields, too, with their purloined power, but weren't able to overcome their instinctive fear enough to use them.

And now, they didn't have the choice, with all their newfound abilities suddenly gone. Mircea could see them through the blue-black darkness, flinching away from blowing orange embers, and looking around in confusion. Could hear them whispering to each other over the crackling flames and the *creak, creak* of another ship about to scupper. Could almost feel the tension in the air as they turned on their dark mage allies, demanding to know what was wrong.

Somebody really ought to show them, Mircea thought, and let loose.

But the flame he hurled this time wasn't a shooting star, it was an inferno, an eruption half as wide as the ship they had congregated on, because it was the only one not yet burning.

Well, until now.

Mircea heard gasps and exclamations from the small crowd that had gathered on the beach, as the mighty torrent of flame snapped like a great whip, exploding the mainmast into a thousand fiery splinters, and killing half the vampires in the process.

The rest of them dove overboard, while the dark mages, after a confused moment, turned their combined fire on Mircea.

Ah, but that was the problem, wasn't it, Mircea thought, jerking the great whip back around, and popping their shields like so many soap bubbles. Joining your power individually meant that each man still stood alone. Whereas he had the combined power of all the witches in the Lagoon, making him virtually invulnerable.

Not that anyone was testing him on it at the moment.

They were too busy burning and jumping and diving and dying, because protection spells do little good when the power of several dozen magic workers hits you all at once.

Mircea glanced behind him, to where Jerome was sitting among a bevy of magical beauties on the side of the overturned hull. And watching the show with stars in his eyes, or at least reflected flames. He was probably thinking how the consul could use the spell, aptly called Lover's Knot, to transfer the power of any magic workers she chose to her vamps.

All that was needed was for the witches to fall in love.

Mircea didn't know how, but the spell used affection to tie a knot in two people's power, allowing each to use the talents of the other. That was why the witch had been able to drain him earlier. Her lover was a master vampire, so when she'd borrowed his power, she had essentially acted as a master, too. Meanwhile, the vamp had been able to run amuck with her magic.

Like Mircea was currently doing.

Of course, she had been an accident. He had stolen her affections, no doubt engendered by vampire mental manipulation in the first place, when his befuddled mind mistook her for Dorina. Giving him access to her power, when a new knot was formed.

The other witches, however, had been on purpose. For someone with his abilities, it had been easy to unravel the knots connecting them to the enemy vamps and to reconnect them to him instead. Leaving him with access to all of their power.

"Mircea!" Jerome said, drawing his attention to the group of mages battling with Hieronimo's people near the beach. It didn't look like they were as intent on continuing the fight as making it to shore, but that wouldn't do. These men had information their side needed, and couldn't be allowed to escape into the city.

"Ladies," Mircea murmured, and explained the situation to the one Italian in the group.

A moment later, he was almost run down by a gaggle of girlish enthusiasm, as the witches jumped into the water and hurried to the aid of Hieronimo's people. And thereby also delivered themselves into their hands, just as the mage had wanted. Sometimes, Mircea thought, watching the girls gleefully lay waste, things actually worked out.

And then he went back to lashing the surfacing vampires some more.

❖ ❖ ❖

"Dory! Dory!"

I awoke to pounding, the smell of sizzling meat, and a weird, high-pitched whine. The first was due to the spells the mages were lobbing at the ward. It seemed they'd given up trying to bypass the system and were attempting to bring it down the old-fashioned way. And from all the bouncing around it was doing, visible whenever another brightly colored spell hit it, they appeared to be succeeding.

The second distraction was on our side, as the babies threw themselves at their own shield, desperate to break through. Not because they were scared; they were too far gone to be scared. But because they were *hungry*.

I stared at them, my brain trying to play catch-up even as somebody continued shaking me.

And then I got it, threw off Marlowe's hold, and scrambled to my feet.

I still didn't know where the weird whine was coming from, but it wasn't the shield over Louis-Cesare's cell, which was down. And he was out and on his feet, if you counted being supported by Anthony. Marlowe must have fed him, because there was blood around his mouth where there had been none before, although it hadn't made any noticeable improvement.

And no way could he fight like that.

I met Marlowe's eyes, and the look on his face told me exactly how much trouble we were in. "Have a nice nap?" he asked, but for once, it wasn't sarcastic.

It was hopeful.

"Yeah," I said, glancing at the babies again. "Yeah, I did."

And then the whine amped up a couple hundred notches, as the ward separating us from the horde outside started to make a sound like every car on the block had decided to screech around a corner at the same time.

Marlowe cursed and grabbed me. And I suddenly found myself inside the small cell where Louis-Cesare and Anthony had been imprisoned, along with them. Our backs hit the wall courtesy of a freaked-out Marlowe, who shoved us inside and then all but flew to the box on the wall.

And before I could ask what the hell, he was slamming into the bricks beside me.

"This one's on me; next one's yours!" he shouted cryptically, while staring past me at the ward.

And then not staring at it, because a second later it was gone, blowing out in a blast of wind and sound, and an army was rushing in at us.

I started forward to meet them, because what other choice was there? Only to have Marlowe jerk me back. Right before the wave of guards slammed into the invisible barrier around the cell, snarling and cursing, and in one case, bursting into flame.

Okay, I thought. I guess I knew what Marlowe had been doing at the box. Only I didn't see how that helped us, since the re-engaged shield on the cell wasn't doing anything but pissing them off. And wasn't going to last, if that box contained what I thought it did.

And I guess Anthony felt the same. The next moment, he was grabbing the two of us and all but cracking our heads together, because he was pissed. "The talisman is outside!" he snarled, gesturing at the box. "Those damned mages will just deactivate—"

"Those damned mages are about to be busy," Marlowe snarled back and shoved him down.

"What the hell?" Anthony said, looking like a guy who hasn't been manhandled in a while.

And then like one who'd decided he could live with it when the whole room suddenly lit up, like the sun had dropped in for a visit.

I didn't see what was happening because my vision all but whited out. And because I'd instinctively shut my eyes and ducked my head, along with everyone else. For a long second, the four of us were just hunkered down in the middle of the cell, while what sounded like a hundred individual explosions took place outside, and a hundred voices screamed—

And then cut off abruptly, when the sun went nuclear.

The talisman, I thought. They were the battery packs of the supernatural world, gathering Earth's magical energy and storing it for later use. There must have been one in the box, powering the shields and whatever else needed power down here. And which was currently releasing it all at once, because Marlowe, the crazy bastard, had overloaded it.

I did glance up after a moment; I couldn't help it. And saw a bunch of dark bodies being thrown around like ping pong balls, visible only when they hit our shield, and even then only as shadows against the boiling yellow-white light. Saw them ripped apart as the ward's final explosion tore through the room, expending its power in a hurricane of brilliance and sound. Saw

—

Nothing.

Because there was suddenly nothing left to see. Our shield gave up the ghost a few seconds after the conflagration, with a small sigh. It didn't hold much power itself, and there was suddenly nothing left for it to draw on. But it had held out long enough to protect us—and no one else.

I stared through leaping aftereffects at a room washed clean of everything, including the attacking vamps. Who were only there in the form of the bloody, burning mess splattering walls, floor, and ceiling, and still sizzling. It was a hell of a sight, I thought dizzily.

And then the babies attacked.

Their shield had dropped along with ours, and now they were coming, blood-maddened and furious, in a scramble of wild eyes and crazy, electrocuted hair. And were stopped abruptly by the hand Marlowe flung out, pausing them the same way that Radu had the vicious tot at Louis-Cesare's court. Like him, they stayed a few feet away, thrashing and snarling and spitting, while Marlowe looked at me, breathing a little hard.

"All right. Your turn."

"What? What?" Anthony was spluttering and staring about, apparently just realizing what Marlowe had done. And then clapping him on the back, almost causing him to lose control of the infants. "You mad son of a bitch! You did it!"

"I cleared this room and the space outside," Marlowe corrected him. "Nothing more."

"What?"

"It will be flooded with guards again momentarily—"

"*What?*"

"Well, it didn't kill those upstairs, did it?" Marlowe asked, but he was still looking at me.

"Then you didn't do a damned thing!" Anthony yelled. "We're still stuck down here!"

"Not for long," I said, because Marlowe was right.

It was my turn.

I grabbed Louis-Cesare.

He may have had a meal, but he didn't look like it. The blue eyes were dazed and struggled to focus. The pale face was not so much white as blue-white, with dark shadows the only color left besides those brilliant blue eyes. If anything, he looked worse than before.

"Are you able to pull from family yet?" I asked, really hoping that was why Marlowe had fed him.

"Starting to," he said hoarsely.

"Okay, good. But right now, I need you to stop and concentrate on—"

"Stop?" That was Anthony again. "What do you mean, stop? He needs to get his power back! He needs—"

"To listen!" I said, and pushed Anthony aside, because it was either that or belt him. "You need to focus on them," I told Louis-Cesare, and gestured at the babies. "You need to make them love you."

"What?" Anthony said. "What the hell are you—"

Marlowe decked him. A quick uppercut that didn't injure him, but only because very little could injure Anthony. The durability of a damned tank was one of his master's powers, which was why he looked a lot sturdier than Louis-Cesare, despite probably being treated the same. However, it did drop him.

He stared up in confusion and no little surprise. "Kit! Have you lost your damned mind?"

"Shut up!" Marlowe told him and looked at Louis-Cesare. "Do what she says. Do it now!"

But Louis-Cesare didn't understand. He wasn't usually slow on the uptake, but it had been a hard week, and his body was using all the blood he'd obtained to try to heal. It didn't look like a lot was left over for figuring out crazy long shots.

He finally gave up and just addressed the request itself. "I don't..." he stopped, swallowed, and tried again. "I don't have your father's gifts—"

"You don't need them. Any vampire can do it. Half of them turn on the charm to feed," I reminded him urgently.

"But they're babies." He looked at them blearily. "What can they possibly—"

"Trust me. Just trust me. *Please.*" I didn't have time to

explain, and I doubted that, right now, he'd have understood anyway. Luckily, he didn't ask anything else. Didn't bitch or complain. Didn't demand a ton of information so that he could judge the situation, because I was only a little woman and couldn't be trusted.

He just looked at the babies and whispered a suggestion.

It was soft, sweet, and seductive. It was also eye-opening because I'd never seen him do that before. He hadn't exactly needed it with me, and I strongly suspected that he was too proud to want any woman he'd have to mentally overwhelm, anyway. But he could have.

Oh, yeah, he could have, I thought, basking in just the overflow.

Some of the babies were starting to calm down as well and were looking around, seemingly confused. Others were starting to claw harder, trying to get to him, but whether to kiss or to kill, I wasn't sure. And still more appeared unfazed.

The only thing they lusted after was blood.

"This isn't working," Marlowe said tightly.

"You need to up the power," I told Louis-Cesare urgently, because some vamps were starting to reappear outside.

And he tried. I could see the veins standing out on his neck, the pulse pounding at his temple—and the desperation in his eyes because he hadn't had time to heal. He wasn't strong enough.

"I don't... have your father's gift," he repeated, panting.

"You don't need it—"

Wild blue eyes met mine. "Right now, I do!"

"You *don't*." My hands found the sides of his face and pulled him down to me. "You don't need his power; you already have mine. You have *Dorina's*. We're linked, remember?"

I didn't know if he understood. Didn't know how much of that had gotten through to a mind still reeling from days of torture and blood loss. Didn't know anything because the room was suddenly inundated with a new wave of attackers, slipping and sliding on the blood of the first.

And being met by my last potion bomb, activated by a scream as I spun to meet them, because I couldn't reach my pack. But I didn't need it. It was still lying in the middle of the floor, under their feet as they tore inside.

And then floated up into space, because gravity had just been jerked out from under their feet.

The effect spread into the outer room as well, sending the vamps trying to get through the door tumbling backwards toward the stairs, like astronauts horsing around on the space station. But that was actually a bad thing, because the farther the bomb's effects spread, the faster they would dissipate. We were looking at seconds here.

So I grabbed the vamps floating nearby, shoved them out of my way, and used the momentum to struggle toward my pack. It was wafting up into the air now, too, only to be grabbed by a vamp right before I could reach it. Who jerked it away from me so hard he went spinning around helplessly. And then flipping over as I snatched it back and pushed off him, all at the same time. Because I don't buy weapons that I don't know how to use!

Another vamp grabbed me and got a knife in his eye for his trouble. Blood went spurting everywhere in a lazy cascade of droplets, making me almost blind. Until I shoved off the floor to get above them, and went zooming toward the ceiling—

And then abruptly crashed back down to Earth.

But not because my purchased magic had suddenly given way.

But because somebody else's had voided it.

Jonathan, I thought, looking up from the bloody ground. I saw the cold smile that never reached colder eyes. I saw a hand raise, and lips open for a curse—

And then I was being trampled by a rush of boots and tennis shoes and hard high heels suddenly stabbing down all around me.

But not from Jonathan's vamps, I realized after a second.

But from *ours*.

And the best thing—the very best thing—was that no one

on their side got it. They had the spell; they knew what it could do. But apparently, it had never once crossed their minds that the lab rats they'd made were anything to worry about. Probably thought they were just panicked by the battle and were trying to get out.

And they kept right on thinking it, until the baby vamps starting ripping off heads.

Because the babies weren't babies anymore. Or, rather, they were, but they were also in a Lover's Knot with a first-level master. One who might be too weak to pull much from the family right now, but who was perfectly able to open a conduit for them to do so. The spell bestowed his talents on them, and the family donated all the power they needed to use them.

Making them suddenly look a lot like first-level masters themselves.

By God, I thought dizzily, watching them go.

It was glorious.

And then my own trio of masters were grabbing me, and we were out of there.

CONCLUSION

O h! Oh! There you are!" Elise practically crawled over the airline seat to point out something on the iPad I'd stolen from the European senate. I figured, all things considered, that it was the least they owed me. And I doubted anyone would notice.

It had come from Aagtje's rooms and she had more important things to worry about right now.

Way more.

"Ha!" Elise laughed. "I love that part."

She was talking about the movie currently playing on the little device, showing me and a beautifully coiffed Jacqueline having a dustup at the top of the main stairs of Amour. It had started to rain while we were inside, so all the fleeing guests—and guards, and pretty much everyone else—trying to get away from the maddened horde of first-level masters, had ended up slip-sliding down the magnificent set of stairs. Ridiculous shoes may look cool, but they cause problems when running for your life.

Or fighting for it, I thought, watching a tiny version of me grab tiny Jacqueline's newly shed wedge heel and beat her with it.

Girl hadn't known a lost cause when she saw it. Heinrich had been smarter. He'd left his co-conspirators to take the heat while he headed for something faster than his little sedan chair, namely a black Maserati around the corner.

Of course, that hadn't turned out so well for him, either.

"There she goes, through the window," Elise laughed, because tiny me had just thrown Jacqueline back into Amour, along with her shoes.

"High heels," I told her. "Screw fashion; leave them at home."

She looked like she was taking notes. I guessed she needed them as Heinrich's newly-appointed replacement. Occasionally, Anthony made a good decision; I was assuming it was luck.

Fortunately, Marlowe had stayed behind to help him clean up the mess, maybe to make up for belting him, not that Anthony seemed to hold a grudge. He could be a whiny little bitch at times, but the guy had layers. He was lazy as hell, for instance, but if you ever got him off his ass, he was... fairly formidable, I thought, watching the pad. Where a guy who'd been tortured for a week and drained almost completely dry was nonetheless riding the backs of two scrambling vamps down the stairs, like a goddamned chariot.

Right before he broke both their necks.

"They survived," Elise told me, peering through the seats. "Gave information on a lot of Black Circle ties we didn't know Amour had."

"And won't have for long," I guessed.

She made a happy little grunting sound. Marlowe had opposed Anthony's choice for the new security chief, probably because he still wanted to poach her himself. But he'd agreed to send her to our senate for a crash course on how to properly run her new department anyway. I didn't think he needed to worry; the vamp version of Interpol was more about paperwork than fighting. Elise was going to be fine.

Not that she couldn't do the other, as well, if properly motivated.

"Look, there you are," I said, handing the pad over the seat. I'd already watched it like five times.

The building opposite Amour had been equipped with surveillance equipment, courtesy of the European senate's sneaky new security chief. Unlike her department head, Elise had been concerned about them for some time and had correctly assumed that vamps wouldn't worry about human devices. So now we had a nice, clear copy of the fight, including her come-out-of-nowhere tackle and subsequent pummeling of Heinrich.

"Son of a bitch," I heard her murmur, as the rhythmic sound of his tiny head hitting concrete, over and over and over again, drifted over the seat.

Yeah, she was coming along nicely.

"Champagne?" A very pretty stewardess asked, bending to proffer a tray with two glasses, because I couldn't get up.

I had a vampire in my lap.

Well, his head, anyway.

"Thanks, no," I said, holding up the beer I'd gotten from one of her counterparts. Louis-Cesare didn't even open his eyes. But his hand adjusted my thigh slightly, to make it more comfortable, I suppose.

"That's a bone," I told him. "It doesn't fluff."

Elise handed me the pillow I'd never gotten on our previous flight, and I stuck it under his head. "Better?"

"Perfect." He looked up without opening his eyes and pulled me down for a kiss. "Like you."

I was about to tell him that my leg was asleep and that he needed to sit up. Somehow, I never got around to it. I frowned; I still didn't know what to do with the damned man.

He dozed off, still smiling.

I was about to do likewise, because Anthony had loaned us his personal jet for the return trip, and there was so much room for activities. But Radu came over before I could. And settled in solitary splendor on a huge swivel chair across the aisle, accepting the champagne I'd refused.

"Finally," he told me, with a heartfelt sigh. "Civilization."

"Did you ever round up all the babies?" I asked because that had been his job.

He tossed silky dark hair, which was loose today and extra shiny. It looked like he'd had time for a spa visit before our return. "Oh, yes. It was easy once Claude removed the spell. Good thing, too. If even one had died—" he shuddered and drank champagne.

"It would have been terrible," I agreed. It was bad enough that a bunch of people who didn't want to be vamps in the first place had suddenly found themselves part of a new world—and back to baby status, at that. Because the effects of the spell did not carry over. Anthony had promised to find good homes for them, though, and I thought he meant it. He'd looked genuinely grateful when telling me about it.

He ought to, I thought.

They'd saved his ass.

"More than you know," Radu said, leaning over to pat his son's leg, as if he still couldn't quite believe he was back. It was cute; he'd been touching him all day, I thought, and randomly smoothed away some auburn hair that had fallen in Sleepy's eyes.

"What don't I know?" I asked Radu, who waved over the stewardess. She had acquired some small salmon canapés, topped with crème fraîche and caviar. Anthony knew how to live, I decided, accepting one myself.

Radu shrugged. "What happens to one, happens to both. It's why the spell was never used—by our side, at least."

I frowned and munched salmon. "Weren't they planning to use it to put down some rebellion or other?"

He nodded. "A group of rogue mages came up with the idea five hundred years ago, distorting an old torture spell created sometime in the Middle Ages. They used it in battle with the consulate forces with great effect—and the consul fully intended to do the same. But Hieronimo's mages took it from the witches and refused to recreate it. And since the only men who knew it were dead by then..." he shrugged.

I frowned harder. Because I knew the consul. "And she didn't... press the issue?"

"Not after they explained that you can't divorce the ability to share magic from the requirement to share fates. If a vampire is linked to a mage—or another, higher level vamp in our case, and one of them dies..."

"They both do." I felt my lips suddenly go numb.

In all the chaos, I hadn't stopped to think about what would happen to Louis-Cesare if even one of those babies was killed. Not that I saw an alternative to what we'd done: we'd been outnumbered and outgunned by something like five hundred to one. And nobody's that good.

But still…

I swallowed and ran my hand through the thick, soft hair some more.

I was really glad I hadn't thought about it.

"Yes, they both do," Radu said. "Or however many you have in a grouping, because as you saw, it is possible to link multiple people into the spell. But then you greatly increase the chances that the entire group will die. The visions you saw were of a shipment of witches going to the rebellion, which had stopped in Venice for provisioning before heading to the war. They were needed because the previous ones had died when their vampire counterparts did."

"But I thought the consul was losing—"

"She was, for a time. But losing doesn't mean you inflict no casualties on the other side, and every time one of the linked vampires went down, they lost a witch. So they constantly needed new ones, and the continued raids allowed some of her people to track them to Venice."

"Where they got help from Hieronimo's people and Mircea."

Radu nodded. "He didn't understand the risk he was taking at the time. If even one of the witches he had linked himself to had died, so would he. Fortunately, the rebels had chosen them well, and the women were all fairly capable from what he tells me."

I flashed on a moonlit sea, angry clouds above, and snapping spell fire below. And a bunch of dark mages who had looked like they wished they'd chosen differently. I grinned. You go, girls.

"But it still feels like the spell could be used in battle," I said, because it was a hell of a thing, seeing vampires and witches swap power.

"It can be, as Jonathan just demonstrated. But at a heavy price."

Jonathan, I thought, and saw my hand clench in Louis-Cesare's hair before I ordered it to let go. I'd been looking for the slimy son of a bitch when I ran into Jacqueline. And by the time I handed her her ass, he had disappeared. Once again.

But I didn't think we'd heard the last of him.

He definitely hadn't heard the last of me.

"The consul has Kit looking for places the other side could find witches," Radu said. "The Silver Circle protects much of the magical community, of course. But some of the far-flung covens could be a problem."

"That's what happened last time," I said, remembering. "The rebels' dark mage friends could have volunteered themselves for the spell, but they weren't going to put their lives in the hands of a bunch of vamps. So they kidnapped witches they didn't care about instead."

Radu nodded. "Typical. Of course, all this was before my time, so I only know what Mircea told me this morning, when we spoke. You probably know more about it than I do. Dorina's mental gifts are impressive."

"He did it all for her," I said, thinking back.

"For you," Radu corrected, a hand on my knee. "He did it for both of you."

He patted me gently, then got up to watch the movie with Elise. "Oh, yes," he said, after a moment. "There's nothing quite like a stiletto heel, is there?"

"Dory said not to wear them in combat."

Radu sighed. "My dear. When it comes to fashion, don't listen to anything Dory says."

I smiled and drifted off.

This time, I didn't dream.

The End

ALSO BY KAREN CHANCE

The Cassie Palmer Series

Touch the Dark

Claimed by Shadow

Embrace the Night

Curse the Dawn

Hunt the Moon

Tempt the Stars

Reap the Wind

Ride the Storm

Brave the Tempest

Shatter the Earth

Ignite the Fire: Incendiary

Ignite the Fire: Inferno

Hijack the Seas: Seismic

Hijack the Seas: Tsunami

The Midnight's Daughter Series

Midnight's Daughter

Death's Mistress

Fury's Kiss
Shadow's Bane
Queen's Gambit
Time's Fool
Fortune's Blade

The Lia de Croisset's Series

Junk Magic
Weird Magic

Standalones

Masks (Mircea Basarab)
Siren's Song (John Pritkin)

CONNECT WITH ME

Follow me on Twitter: https://twitter.com/CasPalmerSeries

Friend me on Facebook: https://www.facebook.com/
#!/KarenChanceBooks

Subscribe to my blog: http://
www.karenchance.com/news/news

www.ingramcontent.com/pod-product-compliance
Lightning Source LLC
Chambersburg PA
CBHW070332130626
46556CB00007B/2825